學科能力測驗、指定科目考試、全民英檢中級/中高級適用
亦可搭配十二年國教課綱加深加廣選修課程「英文作文」

英語 Make Me High 系列

WRITE RIGHT, NO NG

英文這樣寫，不NG

張淑媖　應惠蕙　編著
車畇庭　審定

三民書局

國家圖書館出版品預行編目資料

英文這樣寫，不NG / 張淑媖,應惠蕙編著;車昀庭
審定.－－初版三刷.－－臺北市: 三民, 2019
面；　　公分.－－(英語Make Me High系列)

ISBN 978-957-14-6276-9　（平裝）
1.英語 2.寫作法

805.17　　　　　　　　　　　　　106002355

© 英文這樣寫，不NG

編 著 者	張淑媖　應惠蕙
審 定 者	車昀庭
責任編輯	張玲嘉
美術編輯	黃顯喬
發 行 人	劉振強
著作財產權人	三民書局股份有限公司
發 行 所	三民書局股份有限公司
	地址　臺北市復興北路386號
	電話　(02)25006600
	郵撥帳號　0009998-5
門 市 部	(復北店)臺北市復興北路386號
	(重南店)臺北市重慶南路一段61號
出版日期	初版一刷　2017年3月
	初版三刷　2019年9月
編　　號	S 801090

行政院新聞局登記證局版臺業字第○二○○號

有著作權・不准侵害

ISBN　978-957-14-6276-9　（平裝）

http://www.sanmin.com.tw　三民網路書店
※本書如有缺頁、破損或裝訂錯誤,請寄回本公司更換。

序

英語 Make Me High 系列的理想在於超越，在於創新。

這是時代的精神，也是我們出版的動力；

這是教育的目的，也是我們進步的執著。

針對英語這種國際語言的全球化趨勢，

我們設計了此套功能取向的英語學習叢書。

面對英語，不會徬徨不再迷惘，學習的心徹底沸騰，

心情好 High！

實戰模擬，掌握先機知己知彼，百戰不殆決勝未來，

分數更 High！

選擇優質的英語學習叢書，才能激發學習的強烈動機；

興趣盎然便不會畏懼艱難，自信心要自己大聲說出來。

本書如良師指引循循善誘，如益友相互鼓勵攜手成長。

展書輕閱，您將發現…

學習英語原來也可以這麼 High！

給讀者的話

「聽、讀」是被動的接收,「說、寫」是主動的表達。「說、寫」表達能力好,意思才能互相溝通。寫是透過文字的表達,使想法傳達層面更廣、更長遠,影響更深。本書《英文這樣寫,不 NG》針對這個理念提供一般高中生紮實的練習,對於大考寫作能有完善的準備,對於一般日常英文寫作也可以駕輕就熟。同時,對於英文寫作有興趣或需要學習書寫英文之人士,本書也提供基本寫作的技巧,讓您寫作順暢不 NG。

本書每個單元包括:1) 說明 2) 舉例 3) 範文 4) 轉折語的介紹和練習 5) 層次的練習 6) 作業練習。從片段到整體,融合理論和實際運用,達到寫作的目的,甚至獲得寫作的成就感。

寫作除了技巧,更重要的是,內容與表達言之有物才能使人信服。言之有物必須靠多看、多讀、多想,必須用足夠的英文詞彙表達想法。本書提供完整的寫作觀念和方法,也教導如何腦力激盪 (Brainstorming) 讓讀者開啟更多想法,使內容更豐富。Practice makes perfect. (熟能生巧),只要跟著本書按部就班練習,並自己努力增加英文詞彙,一定可以寫出「不 NG」的文章,創造「不 NG」的生活。

張淑娸

「英文寫作」對大部分的高中學生甚至老師而言,都是聽、說、讀、寫四種能力中最困難的,因為並非英文好就表示有能力寫出一篇好文章。而且,英文寫作佔分比例重,近年來題型也更為多變。因此,老師與學生都應以更加嚴謹的態度看待英文寫作。

筆者二十多年的教學生涯中,發現學生在下筆時,經常腦中一片空白,寫出來的文章也不符合英文架構,所以本書以循序漸進的方式,先從加長句子,熟悉英文作文架構,再進而針對不同類型的文體,教導學生如何進行腦力激盪、寫出主題句和結論句,並善用轉折詞,以培養學生先有能力寫出一篇簡單但文法結構均正確的段落文章。在建構於此基本能力上,提升作文中的用字精確度、變化句子結構並豐富文章內容，以寫出更有深度的作文。

為達成上述教學目標，《英文這樣寫，不 NG》內容涵蓋所有的作文型態，由淺入深，清楚明瞭，相信是英文寫作自學與老師教學的最佳教材。

應惠蕙

寫作是需要系統性訓練的一種思考及書寫能力。和聽與說不太相同，即便有一個很好的語言環境，一般人也很難自然成為一個能寫的人。每每受邀演講和寫作相關的主題時，我總請自認為自己中文寫的不錯的聽眾舉手，至今演講超過數百場，充滿自信舉手的聽眾不超過五人！對母語的寫作尚且如此，更遑論外語！

如果如此困難，可不可以就不要學了呢？很不幸的，答案是「當然不行！」因為每一個語言在書寫上都有其邏輯、句構、敘事的方式、整體的架構和標點符號的用法。有一些在各語言中或許相通，但很多是非常具有獨特性的！也就是說，若沒有掌握這個語言寫作的基本規則，就不算掌握了這個語言獨特的思考邏輯及有效的溝通方法，而學習也就功虧一簣了。

既然非得學，那就要找到好的工具書幫助妳 (你) 學好！

這一本書是三個教學資歷加總超過 80 年的英文老師，在反覆討論、思辯、推敲英文寫作可以教什麼、要如何教、如何安排順序的結晶。因此，妳 (你) 們可以看到我們對寫作的想法和實踐的方法。更重要的是，這是一本循序漸進，從學習者的需求出發來編寫的寫作練習書。

我自己很喜歡這一本書，也希望妳 (你) 們發現它的實用！

車昀庭

Contents

Sentence Expansion

To write a good paragraph, you have to be able to write good sentences first. By making your sentences longer, you can not only make them more interesting but also help your readers better "see" what you are writing about. The first step to reach this goal is to add more information to your sentences, especially by using adjectives and adverbs. Follow the example below and make a short sentence become a more informative one by expanding it.

Example

Who	**The cat** is eating.
What kind	The **cute black** cat is eating.
How	The cute black cat is eating **hungrily**.
Where	The cute black cat is eating hungrily **in the kitchen**.
When	The cute black cat is eating hungrily in the kitchen **right now**.
Why	The cute black cat is eating hungrily in the kitchen right now **because it hasn't eaten anything for two days**.

In the above example, the sentence has been expanded according to the following steps:
1. Add adjectives to describe the subject.
2. Add adverbs to describe the verb.
3. Add an adverbial phrase about the place.
4. Add an adverbial phrase about the time.
5. Add an adverbial phrase or clause about the reason.

Exercise A

Now it's your turn to expand your sentences. Try your best to make your sentences interesting.

Who	*The bird* flew.
What kind	

How	
Where	
When	
Why	

參考答案請參閱解答本 p. 1

In addition to the above ways to expand your sentences, you can also use coordinating conjunctions (對等連接詞) like *and*, *but*, *or*, etc., to make your sentences longer.

Examples

- Jack thanks Ms. Smith **and** goes to his locker.
- You can keep your books inside your locker **or** carry them with you.
- It is the classroom which you have to go to at the beginning of your school day, **but** you will need to go to different classrooms for different classes later.

Exercise B

Now, try to expand the following sentences with the given coordinating conjunctions.

1. On the hall walls, Jack saw many sports medals. (*and*)

   → _____

2. Do you want to meet me in the cafeteria for lunch? (*or*)

   → _____

3. I'd be glad to play basketball with you. (*but*)

   → _____

參考答案請參閱解答本 p. 1

In addition to using coordinating conjunctions to make your sentences longer and more interesting, you can also reach the goal by using subordinating conjunctions (從屬連接詞), relative pronouns (關係代名詞), and appositives (同位語).

📖 Examples ▶

- **Since** we were frightened of being caught, we escaped at the sound of the broken glass.

  (→ *using a subordinating conjunction to begin an adverbial phrase*)

- I made up my mind to save the money **which** I made from delivering newspapers.

  (→ *using a relative pronoun to begin a relative clause*)

- Ken, **an Asian boy,** is standing next to Jack's locker.

  (→ *using an appositive*)

✏️ Exercise C

Now, try to make the following sentences longer by adding a relative pronoun, an appositive, or a subordinating conjunction. The first one has been done for you.

1. The stones looked just like comets. (*that*)

   → *The stones looked just like comets that fell from the sky.*

2. Peter lives next to my grandmother. (*an appositive*)

   → _____

3. I can totally understand your feelings. (*because*)

   → _____

4. I discovered an envelope inside the bag. (*after*)

   → _____

參考答案請參閱解答本 p. 1

Next, follow the given steps to write longer sentences.

1. Think of a simple sentence.
2. Think of some adjectives and adverbs which can modify the words in the simple sentence, and then write them down.
3. Make the sentence longer by using the adjectives and adverbs that you just thought up and wrote down.
4. Think of some prepositions and write them down.
5. Make your sentence longer and more informative by using the prepositions that you just thought up and wrote down.
6. Think of some conjunctions, and write them down.
7. Make your sentence even longer by using the conjunctions that you just thought up and wrote down.

Exercise D

I. *Fill in the following blanks with the words from the box below. The first one has been done for you.*

> greeted   crept   letter

1. The lady ___*greeted*___ the boy.
2. The thief _____ into the house.
3. The man wrote a _____ .

參考答案請參閱解答本 p. 1

II. *Think of some adjectives and adverbs that can expand the sentences above, and write them down below.*

_____

參考答案請參閱解答本 p. 1

III. *Use the adjectives and adverbs above to make the sentences longer. Follow the example below.*

Example:

· *The lady greeted the boy.*

→ *The **old** lady **warmly** greeted the **young** boy.*

1. _____

→ _____

2. _____

→ _____

參考答案請參閱解答本 p. 1

IV. *Think of some prepositions and write them down.*

_____

參考答案請參閱解答本 p. 1

V. *Use the prepositions above to make the sentences that you've written above longer and more interesting. Follow the example below.*

Example:

· *The old lady warmly greeted the young boy.*

→ *The old lady warmly greeted the young boy **in front of** her house.*

1. _____

→ _____

2. _____

→ _____

參考答案請參閱解答本 p. 1

VI. *Think of some conjunctions and write them down.*

參考答案請參閱解答本 p. 1

VII. *Use the conjunctions above to make the sentences that you've written above even longer. Follow the example below.*

Example:

· *The old lady warmly greeted the young boy in front of her house.*

→ *The old lady warmly greeted the young boy in front of her house **as** he passed her the local daily newspaper, **but** he didn't feel comfortable in her presence.*

1.
→

2.
→

參考答案請參閱解答本 p. 1

Unit 2

Brainstorming

2-1 Clustering

Clustering (群集) is a way to brainstorm ideas. It shows the links among your ideas by using circles and lines.

To cluster, follow the steps below:

1. Write your topic in a circle in the center of a piece of paper.
2. Write any ideas you have about the topic in circles around the central circle, and join these ideas to the main topic with a line.
3. Write more related ideas in circles around the first circle, and then join these new circles to their matching ideas.
4. Then repeat the same process to the second, third, or all ideas.
5. The idea which has the most circles joined together is usually the topic that you should write about.

Example

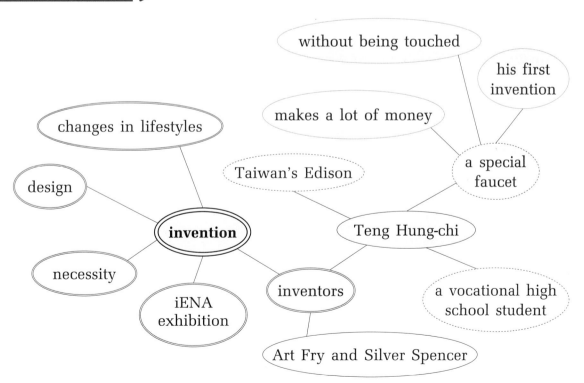

After clustering, you may choose the ideas that you want to write about.

📖 Example ▷

· invention → inventors → Teng Hung-chi

→ a special faucet $\begin{cases} \text{his first invention} \\ \text{without being touched} \\ \text{makes a lot of money} \end{cases}$

Next, you can write a simple topic sentence from these ideas.

📖 Example ▷

· Teng Hung-chi invented a special faucet.

Now, add some adjectives, adverbs, prepositions, conjunctions, etc. to make your topic sentence longer.

📖 Example ▷

· Teng Hung-chi, a famous Taiwanese inventor, invented a special faucet which could run automatically without being touched when he was 17.

✎ Exercise

Now, practice clustering on the topic of holidays.

参考答案請參閱解答本 p. 1

2-2 Listing

Brainstorming can help you come up with many ideas. In addition to clustering, listing is also a good way to brainstorm. To do this, make a list of all the ideas you can think of about a certain topic. The list can be words, phrases, or sentences.

Here are some tips to follow.

1. Write down a certain topic on a piece of paper.
2. List every idea about the topic that comes to mind.
3. Don't stop writing, even though some of these ideas might not seem to be good enough.
4. Keep going until you run out of ideas.

Example

Topic: Hobbies

Ideas:

- listening to music
- watching magic shows on weekends
- biking
- shouldn't play video games all the time
- going to the movies with friends
- playing the piano
- going mountain climbing
- TV programs are getting worse

Exercise

Choose one of the following topics: sports, travel, music, or food. Brainstorm and list all the ideas that you can think of about the topic.

Topic: _____

Ideas: • _____

• _____

• _____

• _____

• _____

參考答案請參閱解答本 **p. 1**

Unit 3

The Topic Sentence

A paragraph is made up of several sentences about the same topic. Out of these sentences, the topic sentence is the most important one in a paragraph. The topic sentence not only introduces the topic but also controls the information that is given in the other sentences of the paragraph. A good topic sentence includes the topic of the paragraph as well as the controlling idea and the writer's attitude (看法) about the topic.

📖 Examples

- **Colors** are everywhere both in our daily routine and everyday conversations!
  topic   *the controlling idea*

- **Friendship** requires many different ingredients.
  topic   *the controlling idea*

✎ Exercise A

Look at each of the following topic sentences and then decide their topic and controlling idea. The first one has been done for you.

1. Colors play a more influential role in your life than you can ever imagine.
   Topic: *Colors*
   The controlling idea: *play an influential role in your life*

2. Exercising every day is good for your health.
   Topic: _____
   The controlling idea: _____

3. Making friends can be like making soup.
   Topic: _____
   The controlling idea: _____

參考答案請參閱解答本 p. 2

Exercise B

Underline the topic and draw a circle around the controlling idea. The first one has been done for you.

1. Excellent inventors get ideas from their own experiences.
2. Colors do spice up ordinary conversations.
3. Mr. Nelson is the teacher that changed my life.
4. Baseball is a sport that most people in Taiwan like.
5. Global warming (全球暖化) has greatly changed the earth's climate.

參考答案請參閱解答本 p. 2

The topic sentence is usually the first sentence in the paragraph, though this is not always the case. A good topic sentence always makes a single point, and it must be clearly stated.

Example

· **Things often have more uses than you could ever imagine**. Some common items that we use every day can seem to perform magic when you know how to use them. Take sugar cubes, for example. You can add one to coffee or tea to make the drink sweet. However, most people don't know that there's another thing that sugar cubes can do—keep cookies crisp!

Exercise C

Underline the topic sentence in each of the following paragraphs.

1. We should always tell the truth. I broke Mr. Wang's window last Sunday, and I didn't tell him about this. Instead of saying sorry to him, I ran away. After that day, I was afraid to look Mr. Wang in the eye. Yesterday, I decided to tell him what had happened. To my surprise, Mr. Wang wasn't

angry. He said he was proud that I had told him the truth. I made up my mind that I would be honest with other people.

2. Here are some easy tips for you to learn how to enjoy opera. First of all, start with short, well-known operas and avoid long, difficult ones. If your first experience is not fun, then you will expect all operas to be boring. Second, learn the story of the opera before you watch it. If you know about the  main characters and the story before you start watching it, it will be much easier to understand what is happening on the stage. Finally, keep an open mind. If you believe that opera can be fun to watch, then you will surely enjoy it.

參考答案請參閱解答本 p. 2

Exercise D

Think of a suitable topic sentence for each of the following paragraphs, and then write each one down in the blanks below.

1. _____ Have you ever thought about why school buses and taxis are painted yellow, and stop signs red? It is because yellow is bright enough to attract people's attention, even in heavy traffic. As for red, it is usually used to indicate warning; as a result, most traffic signs use this color.

2. _____
   _____ The fun person encourages the shy friend; the good listener learns from their smart friends. Everyone feels like they are important because they can help each other in one way or another. This is something that friends who are not as close can't experience.

參考答案請參閱解答本 p. 2

Unit 4

Supporting Sentences

Sentences that add pieces of information to the topic sentence are called supporting sentences. They make the topic sentence more informative, interesting, and convincing. Through supporting sentences, the readers are able to understand the topic better. Unlike topic sentences, which are usually general statements, supporting sentences are more specific statements.

The following are some ways commonly used to support the topic sentence.

1. Giving examples, personal experience, explanations and details
2. Providing historical facts, studies, scientific proof, and statistics
3. Quoting from literature, proverbs, and wise sayings
4. Telling stories or fables

📖 Example A

The topic sentence (1)

Supporting idea 1: giving details (3~5)

Supporting idea 2: giving an explanation (7)

¹Believe it or not, baby oil, medicated oil, or even oil from potato chips can help remove stubborn stains effectively. ²Just follow these steps. ³[First, prepare some baby oil. ⁴Then, put a few drops of the oil on the stain. ⁵Two minutes later, gently wipe it up with some tissues.] ⁶Amazingly, the stained area will look clean again. ⁷[The secret behind the magic is that the organic substances from these kinds of oil can help break down the stains, and thus, make them easier to remove.]

📖 Example B ▶

The topic sentence (1) ⟩	[1]Recent studies show that the level of happiness for most people changes throughout their lives. [2][In a British study between 1991 and 2003, people were asked how satisfied they were with their lives. [3]The result shows a smile-shaped curve (微笑曲線).] [4][Most people lived a happy life when they were kids, and they then become less and less happy as they grow older. [5]For many of them, the worst period in their lives is their 40s. [6]After that, their levels of happiness climb. [7]What's more, men seem to be a little happier than women in their teens, but women become happier than men later in life. [8]The low point seems to last longer for women—throughout their 30s and 40s. [9]When women reach 50, however, their situation improves. [10]Men, on the other hand, have the lowest point in their 40s, going up again when they reach 50.]
Supporting idea: a study and statistics (2~3) ⟩	
Details about the supporting idea (4~10) ⟩	

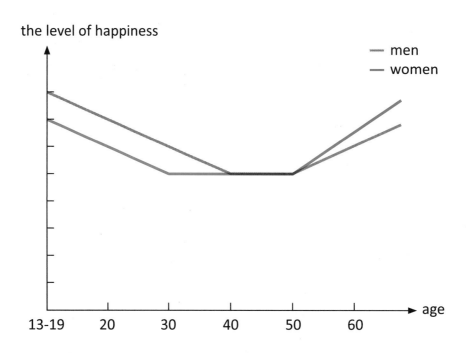

the level of happiness

— men
— women

age

13-19   20   30   40   50   60

Exercise A

*Choose the sentence that does **NOT** support each of the topic sentences.*

( ) 1. It is interesting to go traveling in a foreign country.
   (A) You can see beautiful sights.
   (B) You can learn different customs.
   (C) You can book the ticket before you set off.
   (D) You can meet people from different cultures.

( ) 2. There are several Halloween traditions.
   (A) Halloween is on the last day of October.
   (B) Children go trick-or-treating.
   (C) People use pumpkins to make jack-o'-lanterns.
   (D) Children dress up in special costumes.

( ) 3. Necessity is the mother of invention.
   (A) Many times, people come up with ideas to meet their own needs.
   (B) The solutions to the problems may become great inventions that change our way of life.
   (C) Teng Hung-chi invented a faucet controlled by a built-in sensing device because his hands were so dirty that he did not want to touch the faucet.
   (D) There may be hundreds of failures before something is invented.

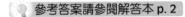

參考答案請參閱解答本 p. 2

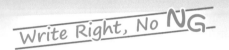

Exercise B

Read the following paragraphs. Underline the topic sentence and write down the sentence number of the supporting ideas. The first one has been done for you.

A. [1]Things often have more uses than you could ever imagine. [2]Some common items that we use every day can seem to perform magic when you know how to use them. [3]Take sugar cubes, for example. [4]You can add a sugar cube to coffee or tea to make the drink sweet. [5]However, most people don't know there's another thing that sugar cubes can do—keep cookies crisp!

Supporting idea 1: *sentence 3~4*

Supporting idea 2: *sentence 5*

B. [1]International trade is the exchange of goods and services between countries. [2]Trade is driven by different production costs in different countries, making it cheaper for some countries to import goods rather than make them. [3]A country is said to have a comparative advantage over another when it can produce a commodity more cheaply. [4]This comparative advantage is determined by key factors of production such as land, capital, and labor.

Supporting idea 1: _____

Supporting idea 2: _____

Supporting idea 3: _____

C. [1]Many patients have reported a decrease in pain after a good laugh. [2]This reduction in pain may result from chemicals produced in the blood. [3]Also, patients might feel less pain because their muscles are more relaxed, or because they are simply distracted from thinking about their pain. [4]It doesn't matter what the truth may be, since there are plenty of people who would agree with the comedian Groucho Marx, who once said, "A clown is like aspirin, only he works twice as fast."

Supporting idea 1: _____

Supporting idea 2: _____

Supporting idea 3: _____

_____

參考答案請參閱解答本 p. 2

Exercise C

Write at least three supporting sentences by giving examples or personal experience for the given topic sentence.

1. For people who live in cities, a fast-food restaurant is a good place to have meals in.

(A) _____

(B) _____

(C) _____

2. These years, Taiwan's birth rate has been decreasing. In fact, Taiwan has the lowest birth rate in the world.

(A) _____

(B) _____

(C) _____

參考答案請參閱解答本 p. 2

Concluding Sentences

A concluding sentence is always at the end of a paragraph, bringing it to an end. Without a clear conclusion, the paragraph will leave readers feeling confused or dissatisfied. A clear conclusion sums up what is already presented, helps the readers have a better understanding of the paragraph and leads them to think about the paragraph once again. Most importantly, the concluding sentence should be related to the main idea of the paragraph.

Some ways to write a concluding sentence are as follows:

1. To state the main idea again by using fewer words.
2. To present a personal opinion.
3. To offer a result, an answer, or a solution.

Example A

- We sometimes lie to cover up our mistakes. While it is true that we make errors from time to time, some of us don't have the courage to admit that we've made them. For example, some students might deceive their teacher about their unfinished homework. They might say that they left it at home when in fact, they didn't even do it. **These students don't want to seem irresponsible, so they make up an excuse—that is, a lie—to save face.**

(→ *The writer presents his personal opinion to explain why people lie as the conclusion.*)

Example B

- When the teenagers are sent abroad, they may have to live alone. Without their parents taking care of them, they are very likely to feel lonely and hang out with some bad friends. Besides, teenagers are always curious. They tend to try something new and strange. Thus, they may be attracted to or get involved in drug use. **Therefore, parents should think very carefully about sending their children abroad.**

(→ *The concluding sentence offers an answer.*)

Exercise A

Choose the best concluding sentence for each of the following paragraphs.

( ) 1. People may sometimes lie to get out of situations that they don't want to be involved in or cannot manage. For instance, if one would rather sleep in on the weekend than go camping with his or her family, the person might give this excuse: "I have had to stay up late recently to finish a company project, so I need to get some rest." This type of lie is also told by students quite often. For instance, students who have been caught cheating on a test might not reveal this to their family. Students may choose not to tell the truth because they aren't confident enough to deal with the anger from their family that they might face. _____

  (A) In short, people who often lie have the habit of sleeping in on weekends.

  (B) When we don't want to face the consequences, lies are convenient ways to avoid such difficulties.

  (C) That is, students who have been caught cheating on a test never reveal this to their families.

  (D) When people are not confident about themselves, they have no choice but to tell a lie.

( ) 2. We sometimes tell "protective lies" so as to keep ourselves out of dangerous situations. Parents may teach their children to use this type of lie in certain circumstances. Some parents, for example, tell their children to say that their mom and dad are too busy to come to the phone if a stranger calls while they are out. _____

  (A) In this way, children may learn the right time to tell lies.

  (B) Besides, they must not tell the stranger where their parents are.

(C) Thus, children should be taught not to pick up the phone when they are home alone.

(D) As a result, protective lies may prevent harm from happening.

(   ) 3. Personal space can be a very sensative issue. For example, have you been irritated by someone standing too close in line, talking too loud or making eye contact for too long? Or, they may have offended you with the loud music from their earphones, or by taking up more than one seat on a crowded subway car. _____

(A) You feel unhappy because your personal space has been violated.

(B) The concept of personal space differs from person to person.

(C) In conclusion, it is useless arguing with impolite people.

(D) Some people easily get angry while others are not.

參考答案請參閱解答本 p. 2

Exercise B

For each of the following paragraphs, try to write down a concluding sentence in your own words.

1. When we were kids, we were taught the virtue of honesty through fairy tales and stories. The story of Pinocchio showed us the importance of telling the truth. The boy who cried wolf finally lost all his sheep as well as the trust of his fellow villagers. _____

_____

2. Nowadays, because of changing ideas, some superstitious customs are being practiced in different ways. People are now turning to artificial feet of a rabbit to take the place of real ones, since this will help to stop the unnecessary killing of animals. However, many people still find comfort in following customs that are based on superstition. _____

3. Some parents believe that watching TV is not good for their children. However, it can be an educational tool. One way to use TV for learning is to watch programs produced specifically for education. Public broadcasting channels have many educational shows for children, and cable TV is full of programs about nature, travel, and  history, which contain many good lessons for children. Additionally, TV shows with subtitles or "closed captioning" for the deaf can help children enlarge their vocabulary and improve their reading ability. Parents can make watching TV with their children into an active activity by asking their children to show their opinions about the show. After the show has finished, parents can also ask children to summarize what has happened.

_____

_____

4. When it comes to communication, many people agree that men and women seem to come from different worlds. For most women, it is important to talk and share feelings with friends. By comparison, men prefer to share facts and specific information. When men are under stress, they tend to keep silent because it is not easy for them to show their emotions.

_____

_____

5. When I was in the first grade in high school, I went to Japan as an exchange student with some of my classmates. We visited schools there and talked to the local students. However, my Japanese was not that good at that time, so I had to talk both in Japanese and in English and a lot of body language as well. I remember we used our heads, hands, and even legs or feet. It was really fun. _____

_____

參考答案請參閱解答本 p. 2

 **Unit 6**

Transitional Words and Phrases

Transitional expressions (轉折詞) serve as bridges between sentences or parts of sentences. They can help readers better understand the relationships between sentences. Transitional expressions fall into different categories (分類) according to the  functions or purposes for which they are used. Transitional words or phrases that are related to supporting and concluding sentences can be categorized as follows:

1. Giving examples:

> for example/instance, in particular, another example/reason is . . . , the first/second/etc. example/reason is . . . , etc.

2. Giving explanations or facts:

> (on one hand) . . . on the other hand, in other words, that is (to say), in fact, actually, etc.

3. Adding more information:

> in addition (to . . .), besides, moreover, furthermore, what's more, what's better/worse, better yet, also, to make matters worse, etc.

4. Showing time order:

> first, second, next, last, finally, to begin with, at the same time, then, etc.

5. Showing a result:

> as a result, therefore, consequently, thus, in this way, needless to say, finally, to be sure, so, etc.

6. Concluding or repeating:

> in sum, to sum up, in conclusion, all in all, that is (to say), in other words, on the whole, to put it differently, in short, in general, generally speaking, etc.

7. Showing proof or information:

according to . . . , based on . . . , (just) as, like, to be sure, etc.

8. Showing contrast:

however, on the contrary, unlike, by/in contrast, by/in comparison, etc.

📖 Example ➡

- The poem also indicates that friendship requires many different ingredients. **For instance**, trust and similar interests are very important.
- **In addition to** trust and similar interests, friendship needs care as well.

Exercise A

Circle the correct transitional expression for each of the following sentences. The first one has been done for you.

1. Unlike most other animals, rabbits touch the ground with their back feet first when they are running. (*Based on*/*Just as*) this fact, many Westerners think this is unusual and regard a rabbit's foot as a lucky sign.

2. Even though Mom and Dad were unable to go with us, we still had a lot of fun in Penghu. (*Finally*/*All in all*), it was a pleasant trip.

3. A positive gesture in one country means something quite different in another from time to time. (*To make matters worse*/*Therefore*), it is better for travelers to get to know a country's culture before they visit it.

4. The Post-it note was not a success at first. (*Also*/*In fact*), it was the result of a failed experiment.

5. There is no such thing as a free lunch; (*that is*/*better yet*), you have to work hard if you want to succeed.

6. Paul never burns the midnight oil. (*More importantly*/*In other words*), he never stays up late studying.

🔖 參考答案請參閱解答本 p. 2

Exercise B

Complete the following paragraph by filling in each of the blanks with the proper transitional expression from the box below.

first   however   thus   for example

A superstition is a belief, and it means that one event may result in—or prevent—another, especially when the two are in no way related. Take a rabbit's foot, ¹_____. Rabbits, unlike most other animals, touch the ground with their back feet first when they are running. Many Westerners think that this is unusual and ²_____ regard a rabbit's foot as a lucky sign. ³_____, there is no scientific proof to support this superstition. Knocking on wood is another similar example. Americans are used to saying, "knock on wood," or actually doing so, to prevent something bad from happening when they have just said it won't occur or hasn't occurred. This is because they are afraid that tree spirits might affect their luck. Many people stick to these beliefs because they often superstitiously associate one event with another.

 參考答案請參閱解答本 p. 2

Exercise C

Complete the following paragraph by filling in each of the blanks with the proper transitional expression from the box below.

(A) However	(B) That is	(C) As a result
(D) Also	(E) For example	(F) On the other hand

It is said that a quick look at our closet can help us to know more about ourselves because the color we often wear indicates what kind of person we are. ¹_____, one afternoon I decided to open up my closet and look inside. I found that I was drawn to my gray clothes—I always believed that I looked great in gray. I had thought that I was willing to share my ideas with others most of the time. ²_____, I have heard that people who like to wear gray clothes seldom have opinions about things around them. ³_____, some reports have indicated that people who wear gray tend to hide their emotions from other people. ⁴_____, it is generally believed that people who are fond of red clothes are full of energy and good at expressing themselves. They are likely

to enjoy getting up early in the morning to start an active day. It seems that they never "feel blue." Are these ideas true? I'm not sure. Still, I think the colors we like to wear are very important. ⁵_____, I believe we will look great and feel good if we wear the colors we like.

参考答案請参閲解答本 p. 2

Exercise D

Complete the following sentences with the given transitional words or phrases.

1. The typhoon brought heavy rain to the small island, and many places there were flooded. *As a result,* _____

2. With my cellphone, I can keep in contact with my friends at all times. *Besides,* _____ *Most important of all,* __ _____ I can always look it up whenever I come across a new word. *All in all,* _____

3. My neighbor, Cindy, works as a volunteer on weekends. She says that she gets happiness out of helping others. *In addition,* _____ _____ *Best of all,* _____

_____

参考答案請参閲解答本 p. 2～3

Unit 7

Punctuation

Punctuation marks (標點符號) are the marks used in sentences to separate meaningful units to help make the meaning clearer.

1. The period (.), the question mark (?), and the exclamation point (!) are used to mark the end of a sentence.

(1) the period (.): used to end declarative sentences (直述句) and imperative sentences (祈使句)

📝 Example

- Stories about individual people tend to attract far more public attention than political events do.

(2) the question mark (?): used at the end of a question or a tag question (附加問句)

📝 Examples

- What makes people choose certain foods over others?
- Almost all the people look forward to holidays, don't they?

(3) the exclamation point (!): used to show emphasis (強調) or to express strong feelings

📝 Example

- She cried out, "Ouch! You are stepping on my toe."

2. The comma (,) has a variety of uses. The following are some common ones.

(1) Commas are often used to separate words, phrases, or clauses.

📝 Examples

- When you read, you have to actively use your memory to recognize words and arrange them into phrases, then sentences, and then ideas.
- Professor Chen can speak French, German, English, and Japanese.

(2) Commas are often used before coordinating conjunctions, such as "and," "or," "but," and "nor." However, in current usage, the comma is often omitted especially in short sentences.

Examples

- Freedom of the press is rightly protected in most democratic societies, but it is just this protection that sometimes allows this freedom to be abused.
- She is a singer, and her sister is a dancer.
- She is a singer and her sister is a dancer.

(3) Commas are used after subordinate clauses (從屬子句), participle phrases (分詞片語) or transposed adverbial phrases (放句首的副詞片語).

Examples

- Though readers enjoy reading about the lives of other people, few of them would like themselves to be the topic of such reports.
  (→ *after a subordinate clauses*)
- Having finished his homework, Jack was allowed to watch TV.
  (→ *after a participle phrase*)
- By working hard, John had his project done in a few days.
  (→ *after a transposed adverbial phrase*)

(4) Commas are often used before and after appositives, nonrestrictive clauses (非限定子句), or inserted (插入的) words and phrases.

Examples

- Tommy, the spoiled child, always has his own way.
  (→ *the spoiled child is an appositive*)
- It was raining hard, which prevented us from going on a picnic.
  (→ *which . . . is a nonrestrictive clause*)
- Education, Dr. Lee insists, has great influence on one's life.
  (→ *Dr. Lee insists is an inserted expression*)

3. The semicolon (;)

Semicolons are used to link independent clauses without coordinating conjunctions. That is, a semicolon may replace a comma plus conjunction or a conjunction.

Examples

- Friendship can't be bought; love can't be bought, either.
- Friendship can't be bought and love can't be bought, either.

4. The punctuation related to transitional expressions:

(1) A comma is used after a transitional expression when it appears at the beginning of a sentence.

📓 Examples

- Numbers may be considered unlucky. **For instance,** 13 is considered unlucky in western superstition. **However,** in Taiwan, the number "four" is viewed as an unlucky number because it sounds like the word for "death."

  (→ *at the beginning of a sentence*)

- In Roman times, people believed that evil spirits might attend a wedding ceremony and hurt the bride. **Therefore,** bridesmaids tried to cheat these unwelcomed visitors by dressing in almost the same way as the bride. (→ *at the beginning of a sentence*)

(2) A comma is used before and after a transitional expression when it is inserted in the middle of a sentence.

📓 Example

- Body language differs from country to county. In Bulgaria, **for example,** people nod their heads to show disapproval.

  (→ *in the middle of a sentence*)

(3) When a transitional expression appears between independent clauses, it follows a semicolon and is followed by a comma.

📓 Example

- A positive gesture in one country can mean something quite different in another; **therefore,** it is better for travelers to get to know a country's culture before they visit the country.

  (→ *Therefore follows a semicolon and is followed by a comma.*)

(4) If a transitional expression is used at the end of a sentence, a comma is used before it and a period is used after it to end the sentence.

📓 Example

- Traffic was extremely heavy; we were delayed, consequently.

  (→ *at the end of a sentence*)

5. The colon (:)

    (1) Colons are used to introduce a list of words, phrases, examples, or explanations.

       📝 Examples

- The rules to abide by in our company are as follows: punctuality, loyalty and hard work.
- The wealthy woman leads a life of luxury: She owns many name-brand bags and drives a sports car.

    (2) A colon is often used to introduce a question or a quotation (引言)

       📝 Examples

- Jeremy was often asked the question: "What made you hold on to your dream of becoming a basketball player?"
- John Kennedy delivered his inauguration address (就職演說) in January 1961. The speech contained the immortal couplet: Ask not what your country does for you; ask what you do for your country.

    (3) A colon instead of a semicolon is used between independent clauses when the second sentence explains or expands on the first sentence.

       📝 Example

- Zack finally had his dream come true: he was appointed CEO of the company.

    (4) Colons are used after a salutation (稱呼語) in a business letter. A comma is used after the salutation for personal correspondence.

       📝 Examples

- Dear Ms. Wang:
- Dear Mary,

6. The dash (—)

    (1) Dashes are used to illustrate specific examples or details.

       📝 Example

- I don't remember when it started annoying me—her hands touching my face that way.

    (2) Dashes are used to give further explanation, just as the use of commas.

📒 **Example**

· Mom had forgiven—and forgotten—long before.

7. The quotation mark (" ")

(1) Quotation marks are used to specify a title, a topic, a song, a program, etc. In this case, the italic (斜體) can be used instead.

📒 **Examples**

· The "Mona Lisa" is one of the most famous paintings in the world.

(→ *to specify a painting*)

· The *Mona Lisa* is one of the most famous paintings in the world.

(2) Quotation marks are used in direct quotations.

📒 **Examples**

· One night, I finally roared, "Don't do that anymore—your hands are too rough!"

· "I'll never forget the experience," said Mary.

(3) Quotation marks are used to indicate words or phrases when they are given a special or unusual meaning.

📒 **Example**

· If you are able to put up with its "unique" smell, you will find stinky tofu very delicious.

8. The ellipsis (. . .): formed by three periods, with a space put between each one

(1) An ellipsis is used to indicate an omission (省略).

📒 **Example**

· Steve Jobs once said, "Your time is limited, so don't waste it living someone else's life . . . Don't let the noise of others' opinions drown out your own inner voice."

(2) An ellipsis is used to show interruption or hesitation, especially in conversations.

📒 **Example**

· Emily: Matt, why don't we buy Mom a pair of jogging shoes for Mother's Day?

Matt: Mmm . . . That sounds good.

Exercise

Fill in the following blanks with the proper punctuation marks. Write "×" if there is no need for any punctuation mark. The first one has been done for you.

1. Sometimes ___,___ the shooting incident seemed close and sometimes far away ____. However ___,___ it was always there in the back of my mind ____.

2. More than a hundred people took the examination _____ only ten passed _____

3. A dumpling looks like a _____ yuanbao (元寶) _____ _____ a type of money used in ancient China.

4. He won the championship _____ as a result _____ he was awarded a gold medal as well as the prize money.

5. The angry lady stood up and shouted _____ "Don't ever call me again _____ "

6. Much to my surprise _____ the living room was tidied up _____ the laundry was done _____ too _____

7. Climbing trees used to be something interesting to do _____ at least to the boys like us.

8. Some tips for improving your memory are as follows _____ set realistic goals _____ cut down on activities that don't require you to think _____ read more _____ and get into the habit of taking notes _____

9. Temperatures change a lot in this area _____ it is like experiencing two seasons in a single day _____ winter in the morning and summer in the afternoon _____

10. What he needs most now _____ in my opinion _____ is our encouragement instead of financial support.

參考答案請參閱解答本 p. 3

Determiners

Determiners (限定詞) are a special kind of adjective. They are used before nouns and are grouped into four types as below.

1. possessives (所有格): my, your, his, her, its, Joseph's, my parents', etc.
2. demonstrative adjectives (指示形容詞): this, that, these, those, etc.
   "This" and "that" are followed by a singular noun, while "these" and "those" are followed by a plural noun.
3. quantifiers (量詞):

Quantifier	Function	Examples
either	one of the two; followed by a singular noun	• There are many food stands on **either** side of the road.
neither	none of the two; followed by a singular noun	• Our host made coffee and tea, but I like **neither** drink.
each	every one of two or many; followed by a singular noun	• **Each** person has <u>his</u>/<u>her</u> own personality.
every	all the members of a group more than two; followed by a singular noun	• **Every** dog has its day.
some	a quantity of whole or a group; followed by either countable plural nouns or uncountable nouns	• I would like to buy **some** books. • It took me **some** time to get the main idea of the reading.
any	every; followed by either countable plural nouns or uncountable nouns, often used in negative or interrogative sentences (疑問句)	• If you need **any** help, please feel free to let me know. • Ms. Warner doesn't have **any** pets.
no	excluding all members of a group; followed by either countable plural nouns or uncountable nouns	• **No** food and **no** drinks are allowed in the library.
much	a great amount of; followed by uncountable nouns	• Hurry! We don't have **much** time left.
many	a great number of; followed by plural nouns	• I'm lucky to have **many** friends around me.

enough	an amount or a number that is as much/many as someone needs or wants; followed by either countable plural nouns or uncountable nouns	• Are there **enough chairs** for everyone?

4. articles (冠詞): a, an, the

"A" and "an" are indefinite articles (不定冠詞), while "the" is a definite article.

📖 Example ▶

• Animal imagery can be found in **many** English expressions, and it has given color to **this** language. For instance, "as quiet as **a** mouse" is commonly used to describe **a** person who is quiet. You can say, "After being caught cheating on **the** exam, Samuel was as quiet as **a** mouse in front of **his** angry parents."

Exercise A

Put "a," "an," or "the" in the following blanks where it is necessary. Mark "✕" if there's no need to put any article. The first one has been done for you.

1. If someone makes a lot of noise, _____*an*_____ elephant would be _____*a*_____ good choice for _____*a*_____ simile.

2. During _____ sale, the customers crowded into _____ mall like _____ herd of _____ elephants.

3. Believe me. _____ English is not as difficult to learn as _____ most people think.

4. This is _____ unusual sort of _____ experience. You were lucky to run into it.

參考答案請參閱解答本 p. 3

Exercise B

Fill in each of the following blanks with a proper determiner in the box below. The first one has been done for you.

> (A) neither (B) much (C) enough (D) any (E) every (F) either (G) no

1. There is a black sheep in ___E___ flock.
2. In the past, there were _____ fish in the lake for both the Thao and the long-haired spirits.
3. The government plans to grow some trees on _____ side of the river.
4. I don't want to be involved in your fight with Richard. I choose to be on _____ side.
5. All the vegetables in our store are grown without using _____ chemicals. You can put your trust in us.
6. I'm _____ fool. I won't believe anything you say.
7. Sandra's parents put _____ pressure on her. They want her to study hard and become a doctor in the future.

參考答案請參閱解答本 **p. 3**

Exercise C

Fill in the following blanks with the correct determiners.

1. 我們決定騎自行車環島旅行。
   → We decided to travel around _____ island by bike.
2. 兩位應徵者都非常優秀，要做出決定並不容易。
   → _____ applicant is very outstanding. It is not easy to make a decision.

3. 我十年前到<u>紐約</u>旅行過一次。

   → I took ＿＿＿＿＿＿ trip to New York ten years ago.

4. 我們暑假讀了兩本小說，兩本都不容易讀懂。

   → We have read two novels in this summer vacation. ＿＿＿＿＿＿ novel is easy to understand.

5. 醫生要他每四小時吃一顆藥。

   → The doctor told him to take one pill ＿＿＿＿＿＿ four hours.

6. Jack 盡各種努力鼓勵 Tiffany，但沒有多大幫助。

   → Jack has made ＿＿＿＿＿＿ effort to encourage Tiffany, but it is not of ＿＿＿＿＿＿ help.

參考答案請參閱解答本 p. 3

Unit 9

Subject-Verb Agreement

1. All singular subjects, except for "I" and "you," take a singular verb, while plural subjects always take plural verbs.

   Examples
   - **This item is** very expensive but useless.
   - In Chinese, **pigs are** traditionally seen as clumsy animals.

2. Collective nouns (集合名詞), such as "class," "family," "group," "police," and "team," are used to name groups. Most collective nouns can be treated as singular or plural.

   Examples
   - **My family has** decided to take a trip to Russia this summer.
   - **The Churchill family have** different plans for the weekend. Mr. and Mrs. Churchill are going to go camping, while their son would like to see a movie with his friends.

3. Nouns, like "children" and "people," are plural nouns. They take a plural verb.

   Example
   - It is a general belief that **people tend** to repeat their mistakes.

4. Some nouns, such as "clothes," "goods," and "pants," are always plural in form and take only a plural verb.

   Example
   - The **pants** I wore today **were** dirty and needed to be washed.

5. Some words that end in "s," such as "the United States," "news," "mathematics," seem to be plural, but, in fact, they are singular. As a result, they take a singular verb.

   Example
   - **The news** that three men were killed in one night **was** really shocking.

6. Some nouns, such as "sheep" or "means," can be singular or plural. Thus, whether this kind of noun takes a singular or a plural verb depends on its number.

   ### Examples

   - The **black sheep** stands out in a flock of white sheep.
   - The eight missing **sheep were** found and returned to their owner.
   - The only **means** to get to the island **is** boating.
   - The **means** to reach the mountaintop **vary**. You can take a bus, a train, or a gondola (纜車).

7. Some nouns, such as "Chinese, Japanese, Swiss," can be singular or plural, while nouns, such as "American" or "German" should add "-s" to form a plural noun.

   ### Examples

   - The **Chinese live** on rice.
   - We have a group of **Germans** staying at our hotel tonight.

8. Numerical (數字的) expressions of time, money, distance, and calculations are taken as a single whole and usually go with singular verbs.

   ### Examples

   - **Ten minutes is** not enough for Jacob to finish his breakfast.
   - **Five hundred dollars is** the price of the book.

9. An adjective following the preposition "the" refers to all people who have the characteristic described, so it should take a plural verb.

   ### Examples

   - **The rich are** not always happy.
   - **The young** today **know** how to fight for their rights.

10. An indefinite pronoun (不定代名詞) is a pronoun that is used to refer in a general way to people and things. Indefinite pronouns have singular and plural forms. A singular indefinite pronoun goes with a singular verb, while a plural indefinite pronoun takes a plural verb.

    (1) Singular indefinite pronouns:

    > either, neither, each, (a) little, much, one, other, another, someone, something, anyone, anything, everyone, everything, nobody, nothing, etc.

Examples

- **Each** of the students in the class **was** given an English name.
- Michelle is always afraid that **nobody likes** her.

(2) Plural indefinite pronouns:

> both, (a) few, many, some, (the) others, several, etc.

Examples

- **A few** of the students **are** sitting in the classroom.
- **Some** cell phone addicts **feel** socially isolated when they can't get access to their cell phone contacts. **Others worry** about not being able to respond to emergencies promptly. Still **others are** psychologically influenced by their cell phones.

(3) Indefinite pronouns that can be singular or plural:

> all, any, none, some, most, etc.

Note that when the noun is uncountable, it should be followed by a singular verb. While the noun is countable, it should be followed by a plural verb.

Examples

- **All** of **the students were** taking the exam in the classroom.
- **Most** of **the money** Tony earned **was** spent on cars.
- **Some** of **the food** the host prepared **was** eaten.

11. When "a lot/lots of," "plenty of," and "a (large/small) quantity/(large/small) quantities of" are used before a plural noun, they require a plural verb. If they are used before an uncountable noun, they require a singular verb.

Examples

- **A lot of time is** needed to complete the report.
- **Plenty of sayings** that include animal imagery **make** English an interesting language.

12. "A (large) number of" is used before a plural noun and requires a plural verb. "The number of" is followed by a plural noun and requires a singular verb.

> **Examples**
> - **A large number of people were** crowding into the mall during the sale.
> - **The number of** fish in the Thao fishermen's nets **was** sharply decreasing.

13. "A (large/small) amount of" and "a great/good deal of" are commonly used with uncountable nouns.

> **Examples**
> - **A large amount of rain has** caused great damage to the area.
> - **A great deal of information was collected** before Ricky wrote his report.

14. When the subjects of a sentence are joined by "and," or "both . . . and . . . ," they are followed by plural verbs in most cases.

> **Examples**
> - Sherry **and** Jerry **have** been best friends since elementary school.
> - **Both** children **and** adults **like** Miyazaki's animated films.

15. When the subjects of a sentence are joined by "(either) . . . or . . . ," "neither . . . nor . . . ," or "not only . . . but also . . . ," the verb(s) should agree with the subject that is closest to the verb(s).

> **Examples**
> - **(Either)** Cynthia **or** her brothers **are** going to the party.
> - **Neither** the students **nor** the teacher **is** cleaning the classroom.
> - **Not only** "Spirited Away" **but also** Miyazaki's other movies **are** popular around the world.

16. Phrases such as "together with," "as well as," and "along with" are not part of the subject. The words that follow these phrases are used to modify (修飾) the subject, so the verb should agree with the subject.

📝 **Examples**

- Christina, **together with** her neighbors, **is** going to visit the exhibition.
- "Spirited Away," **as well as** many of Miyazaki's other movies, **has** hit it big around the world.

17. If the subject of a sentence is an infinitive (不定詞), a gerund or a noun clause, the sentence requires a singular verb.

📝 **Examples**

- To see **is** to believe. = Seeing **is** believing.
- How colors affect appetite **is** something that most people probably do not notice.

18. In a relative clause, the relative pronoun can refer to a singular or plural noun, so the verb must agree with the noun.

📝 **Examples**

- The one who cares about you **loves** you.
- Many sayings that include animal imagery **make** English an interesting language.

Exercise

Fill in each of the following blanks with the correct form of the verb. The first one has been done for you.

1. Fried chicken _____*was*_____ (*be*) my favorite dish when I was little.
2. Peterson and his wife _____ (*own*) a Chinese restaurant, and they spend lots of time managing it.
3. Tim's glasses _____ (*be*) broken when he fell out of a tree.
4. The blind usually _____ (*have*) better hearing than those who can see.
5. The basketball team _____ (*be*) growing more and more excited before the game began.
6. Do you know what Japanese _____ (*like*) to eat?
7. Two times eight _____ (*be*) sixteen.

8. Five minutes _____ (*be*) enough of a break for me.

9. Nobody _____ (*know*) anything about the poet's life.

10. A large amount of treasure _____ (*be*) found in the cave.

11. Both of Dale's sisters _____ (*be*) interested in acting when they were young.

12. Most of the students in this class _____ (*wear*) glasses.

13. A large number of people nowadays _____ (*suffer*) from disconnect anxiety.

14. There are about ten books on the desk. One _____ (*be*) about math, another _____ (*be*) about history, and the others _____ (*be*) dictionaries.

15. Desserts, as well as soft drinks, _____ (*be*) given to children who _____ (*take*) part in the summer camp.

16. Not only Amy but also her classmates _____ (*be*) going on a picnic this weekend.

17. Trick-or-treating, along with putting out jack-o'-lanterns, _____ (*have*) become a traditional Halloween activity.

18. What Emily wants now _____ (*be*) to be left alone for a while.

19. Taking care of her brothers _____ (*be*) what Ariel has to do when her parents are away.

20. Adam talked continuously on the phone and totally ignored Vicky, who _____ (*be*) sitting right in front of him.

參考答案請參閱解答本 p. 3

Unit 10

Avoiding Shifts in Person

A sentence or paragraph is written from a specific point of view: First person (*I* or *we*), second person (*you*), or third person (*he/she/it/one*, or *they*). Keep to the same person when you are writing.

📖 Examples ▶

· To improve <u>your</u> memory, ~~we~~ should change the way ~~we~~ deal with
     you   *you*
information.

· <u>Students</u> who persistently delay doing ~~his~~ assignments usually get further
               their
and further behind with ~~his~~ studies.
        their

✏️ Exercise A

Complete each of the following sentences by circling the correct pronoun. The first one has been done for you.

○ ○ ○ ○ ○ ○ ○ ○ ○ ○ ○ ○ ○ ○ ○ ○ ○ ○ ○

1. For centuries the long-haired spirits lived at the bottom of Sun Moon Lake, and (they/you) had shared the fish in the lake with the Thao.
2. If someone develops the habit of not making an effort to remember things, (*his or her/your*) ability to memorize things will begin to decrease.
3. When moviegoers steep (*ourselves/themselves*) in Miyazaki's films, (*we/they*) easily note three marked characteristics.
4. To save money, you should record every cent you spend. This way, (*we/you*) will know how (*we/you*) *can cut down on waste*.
5. When you hear some key words in a speech, write (*it/them*) down! It may help you to understand the main points better.

💬 參考答案請參閱解答本 p. 3

Exercise B

Complete the following passage by filling in the correct person. The first one has been done for you.

I.

It was a quiet Sunday morning. When ¹ <u>   *I*   </u> was walking in the park, I saw a little boy practicing riding a bike. I thought that it was a dangerous thing for him to do because ² _____ was practicing alone without any adults around. So, I decided to sit on a nearby bench and watch ³ _____ practice. A few minutes later, the little boy suddenly fell off the bike. Luckily, ⁴ _____ was right by his side and soon caught ⁵ _____. As a result, he didn't get hurt. I felt great that day for helping the little boy. I not only helped him but also gained a sense of achievement for myself.

II.

Some people think that most problems with memory are the results of bad habits. For example, if ¹ _____ develop the habit of not making an effort to remember things, your memory will begin to decrease. On the other hand, a good memory can be the result of good habits. To improve ² _____ memory, you should change the way ³ _____ deal with information. Those who have been practicing some memory tips may notice a great improvement in ⁴ _____ memory. However, everyone is unique, and the results may vary from person to person. What works for you may not work for other people. People can always find tips that work best for ⁵ _____.

參考答案請參閱解答本 p. 3

Unit 11

Shifts in Tense

Tense (時態) tells the time when actions take place. Shifts in tense may sometimes be required to indicate changes in time. However, it is best to stick to the same tense in one sentence or from one sentence to another. Shifts in tense without good reason confuse the reader.

1. Shifts in tense are required when changes in time occur in one sentence or between two sentences.

   Examples

   · A dumpling <u>looks</u> like a "yuanbao," which ~~is~~ a type of money used in

     was

     ancient China.

   · I stepped back into the living room and <u>found</u> that the living room ~~was~~

     had been

     tidied up.

2. Shifts in tense should be avoided when there are no changes in time in one sentence or between two sentences.

   Examples

   · I always ~~take~~ the bus when it <u>rained</u>.

     took

   · On New Year's Day, Greeks <u>bake</u> a special type of bread containing a coin made of silver or gold. The person who ~~found~~ the coin in his or

     finds

     her piece of bread will be blessed with good luck for the coming year.

Exercise A

Complete each of the following sentences by circling the correct tense of the verb. The first one has been done for you.

1. Paul laid the book aside and (*picks*/*picked*) up his cell phone to make a call.

2. When my dad was still alive, he always (*teaches*/*taught*) me to help people in need.

3. Though my grandmother is very old, she still (*stays/stayed*) active.

4. A thief broke into my house and (*steals/stole*) a lot of money from my room.

5. Nowadays, many people (*are/were*) deeply involved in online communities.

參考答案請參閱解答本 p. 3

Exercise B

Correct the underlined word in each of the following sentences with the correct tense. The first one has been done for you.

_____*told*_____ 1. Patrick just called and <u>tells</u> me that he was OK.

_____ 2. I had already told you that I <u>will</u> not go to the party last night, so I don't know why you kept waiting for me there.

_____ 3. There used to be plenty of fish in Sun Moon Lake, and there <u>are</u> enough fish for both the spirits and the humans.

_____ 4. After I had finished my homework and was just about to go to bed, I <u>hear</u> a strange sound.

_____ 5. I am positive about the little girl's future, and I <u>had</u> every hope that she will be successful.

參考答案請參閱解答本 p. 3

Exercise C

Complete the following passage by filling in the correct tense of the given verbs. The first one has been done for you.

I.

It was starting to get dark. Although snow flurries [1] _____*drifted*_____ (*drift*) in the dim light of day, Joe could still notice an elderly lady stranded by the roadside. Apparently, she ² _____ (*need*) some help. So, he pulled up in front of her Mercedes-Benz and ³ _____ (*get*) out. When he approached her, she ⁴ _____ (*be*) worried. "No one ⁵ _____ (*stop*) to help for the last hour or so," she ⁶ _____ (*think*) to herself. "⁷ _____ (*be*) he going to rob me?" Realizing that she ⁸ _____ (*be*) frightened, he said quickly, "I ⁹ _____ (*be*) here to help, ma'am. Why don't you wait in the car? It's freezing outside. By the way, my name ¹⁰ _____ (*be*) Joe."

II.

When I ¹ _____ (*be*) shopping at a supermarket one evening, my eye ² _____ (*be*) caught by a boy tugging at his father's sleeve. "Dad, let's get this coffee. With this mark on the package, it ³ _____ (*mean*) the farmers get a fair deal." The child also ⁴ _____ (*pick*) up some bananas with Fairtrade marks on them while talking enthusiastically about how buying this fruit ⁵ _____ (*will*) help banana farmers.

參考答案請參閱解答本 p. 3

Unit 12

Sentence Fragments

A complete sentence has a subject and a verb, and it expresses a complete thought. A sentence fragment is an incomplete sentence with a basic element or some basic elements missing and it doesn't express a complete thought, either. Sentence fragments are very likely to occur in conversation but they are wrong sentences in writing.

1. Common types of sentence fragments

   (1) Noun fragments

   (→ *Only a noun or a noun phrase, without a complete thought*)

   ### Examples

   - All the students in the classroom.
   - The horse meat that is served as a delicacy in certain areas of France.

   (2) Verb fragments (→ *The subject is missing.*)

   ### Examples

   - Have no work to do.
   - John went to a movie left his homework undone.

   (3) Subordinate clause fragments

   (→ *The main clause is missing.*)

   ### Examples

   - If you make an apology.
   - When polar bears are starving due to a lack of food.

   (4) Infinitive and participle phrase fragments

   ### Examples

   - To win the competition.
   - Having worked hard all his life.

2. Revision can be made in different ways based on the context.

   The following are some options to change sentence fragments into complete sentences.

(1) Add the basic element to the fragment: a subject, a verb or a main clause.

Examples

- All the students in the classroom.
  - → All the students in the classroom are concentrated.
- Have no work to do.
  - → I have no work to do today.
- If you make an apology.
  - → If you make an apology, we are sure to forgive you.
- To win the competition.
  - → To win the competition, Jack spent most of the time practicing.

(2) To revise subordinate clause fragments, drop the subordinating conjunction.

Examples

- The horse meat that is served as a delicacy in certain areas of France.
  - → The horse meat is served as a delicacy in certain areas of France.
- When polar bears are starving due to a lack of food.
  - → Polar bears are starving due to a lack of food.

(3) Add a coordinating conjunction to make a compound sentence.

Example

- John went to a movie left his homework undone.
  - → John went to a movie and left his homework undone.

(4) Use participle phrases to avoid verb fragments.

Example

- John went to a movie left his homework undone.
  - → John went to a movie, leaving his homework undone.

Exercise A

Check each of the following sentences. Put an "F" if it is a fragment and put a "C" if it is a complete sentence. The first one has been done for you.

F   1. Because the iPad is so user-friendly and becomes more popular.

_____ 2. The carbon dioxide absorbs the sun's heat and keeps it from escaping back into space.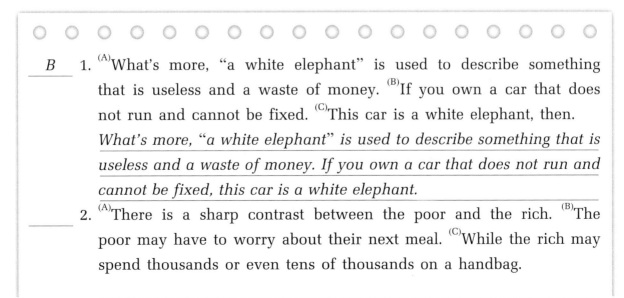

_____ 3. Yuanbao which was a type of money.

_____ 4. If you have the opportunity to visit Taiwan to taste a variety of local foods.

_____ 5. Yesterday, I ran into Miss Lee, my English teacher in senior high.

參考答案請參閱解答本 p. 3

Exercise B

In each of the following passages, there is a fragment. Fill in each blank with A, B, or C that indicates the fragment. Revise the fragment and rewrite the passage. The first one has been done for you.

B   1. (A)What's more, "a white elephant" is used to describe something that is useless and a waste of money. (B)If you own a car that does not run and cannot be fixed. (C)This car is a white elephant, then.

What's more, "a white elephant" is used to describe something that is useless and a waste of money. If you own a car that does not run and cannot be fixed, this car is a white elephant.

_____ 2. (A)There is a sharp contrast between the poor and the rich. (B)The poor may have to worry about their next meal. (C)While the rich may spend thousands or even tens of thousands on a handbag.

3. (A)Getting into the habit of taking notes. (B)Whether you are reading, studying, or listening to a speech, it is useful to write down the information you may want to look up later. (C)In the process of writing down what is mentioned, you are actually organizing information at the same time.

_____

_____

_____

4. (A)*The Annals of Improbable Research*, an American magazine that celebrates the funny side of science. (B)Each year, ten winners are awarded prizes. (C)Most of the award-winning research may seem unusual, but it usually grabs people's attention instead. (D)And no matter how ridiculous the research sounds, people can find it inspiring and amusing.

_____

_____

_____

_____

5. (A)There are several reasons I need to find a roommate. (B)He or she can share the rent. (C)Besides, having someone to talk to. (D)Most importantly, the room would be more like "home" instead of a place to live.

_____

_____

參考答案請參閱解答本 p. 3

Run-on Sentences and Comma Splices

Run-on sentences (連寫句) are two or more independent clauses joined together without conjunctions or the correct punctuation marks. On the other hand, comma splices (逗號誤用) are two or more independent clauses joined together with only a comma or commas. Neither of these types of sentence is correct.

The following five methods can be used to correct these mistakes.

1. Use a period to rewrite the incorrect sentence as two complete sentences. Use this method when the meaning between the independent sentences is already clear.

   Example

   • John Harrison has an enviable job in most people's opinion, he's the official taster for Dreyer's Grand Ice Cream.
     → John Harrison has an enviable job in most people's opinion. He's the official taster for Dreyer's Grand Ice Cream.

2. Use a semicolon when the meanings of the sentence parts are closely related.

   Example

   • In the Chinese language, pigs are traditionally seen as clumsy animals, dogs represent loyalty, wolves indicate violence as well as cruelty, lions are a symbol of authority.
     → In the Chinese language, pigs are traditionally seen as clumsy animals; dogs represent loyalty; wolves indicate violence as well as cruelty; lions are a symbol of authority.

3. Use a coordinating conjunction, such as *and, but, or, nor*, etc. to make the meaning of the sentences clearer.

   Example

   • Because of global warming, large amounts of Arctic ice are melting away, the seal population is falling sharply.
     → Because of global warming, large amounts of Arctic ice are melting away, **and** the seal population is falling sharply.

4. Use a subordinating conjunction to combine the independent sentences. If the subordinating conjunction is added at the beginning of the first independent sentence, this independent sentence is called the subordinate clause. Note that a comma must be used after the subordinate clause. Some of the common subordinating conjunctions are as follows:

Meaning	Subordinating conjunctions
Time	when, while, before, after, as, until, since, etc.
Reason	because, as, since, etc.
Concession (讓步)	though, although, while, even though, etc.
Condition	if, unless, even if, as long as, etc.
Contrast	while, whereas, etc.
Purpose	in order that, so (that), etc.

Examples

Correct each of the following run-on sentences by adding an appropriate subordinating conjunction.

- You are a student, it is a must for you to spend more time studying.
  - → **Since** you are a student, it is a must for you to spend more time studying.

- A woodpecker never suffers any ill effects like brain damage, it has to peck numerous times per day.
  - → A woodpecker never suffers any ill effects like brain damage **even though** it has to peck numerous times per day.

- Knowledge can be acquired from books, skills must be learned through practice.
  - → Knowledge can be acquired from books, **whereas** skills must be learned through practice.

- John works part-time, he wants to save enough money to study abroad.
  - → John works part-time **in order that** he may save enough money to study abroad.

5. Use a transitional expression to separate the run-on sentence into complete sentences. Note that a comma is usually used after the transitional expression. In addition, a semicolon or a period should appear before the transitional expression. Some common transitional expressions are as follows:

Meaning	Transitional expressions
To show result	thus, therefore, hence, accordingly, consequently, as a result, etc.
To show contrast	however, nevertheless, nonetheless, on the contrary, etc.
To explain	besides, moreover, in addition, also, what is more, namely, in other words, that is, etc.
To give examples	for example, for instance, etc.

Examples

Correct each of the following run-on sentences by adding an appropriate transitional expression.

- It had been raining heavily for several days, many low-lying areas were flooded.
  - → It had been raining heavily for several days. **Consequently,** many low-lying areas were flooded.

  - → It had been raining heavily for several days; **consequently,** many low-lying areas were flooded.
- Success belongs to those who work hard, fooling around will get you nowhere.
  - → Success belongs to those who work hard. **In other words,** fooling around will get you nowhere.
  - → Success belongs to those who work hard; **in other words,** fooling around will get you nowhere.

Exercise A

Revise the following run-on sentences according to the given instructions (指示). The first one has been done for you.

1. Harrison's family has been in the ice-cream business for four generations, Harrison himself has spent almost his whole life in it. (*Add a coordinating conjunction.*)

   → *Harrison's family has been in the ice-cream business for four generations, and Harrison himself has spent almost his whole life in it.*

2. The press has a strong influence it can bring about significant changes to the lives of ordinary people. (*Use a semicolon.*)

   → _____

   _____

3. Hsu made this film to indicate that global warming had already become quite serious she hoped that her film could help focus public attention on environmental protection. (*Add a coordinating conjunction.*)

   → _____

   _____

   _____

4. Small islands and low coastal areas could soon be underwater the residents of major cities are likely to have nowhere to live by the end of the 21st century. (*Use a semicolon.*)

   → _____

   _____

   _____

5. It was very hard to find a job more than one hundred applicants were interviewed for five vacancies. (*Use a semicolon.*)

   → _____

   _____

參考答案請參閱解答本 p. 4

Exercise B

Revise the following run-on sentences by adding a proper subordinating conjunction or transitional expression. The first one has been done for you.

1. There is anything you don't quite understand, just let me know and I'll be ready for help.

   → *If there is anything you don't quite understand, just let me know and I'll be ready for help.*

2. You fail a test, you don't have to feel frustrated. On the contrary, you should study even harder.

   → _____

   _____

3. A man can stay alive for more than a week without food, a man without water can hardly live for more than three days.

   → _____

   _____

4. My mom heard what I said, she stepped out of my room without saying a word.

   → _____

   _____

5. Robert is enthusiastic and kind-hearted, he works as a volunteer in the hospital, he donates money to the orphanage regularly.

   → _____

   _____

參考答案請參閱解答本 p. 4

The Format of a Paragraph

The first step in writing a paragraph is to use the correct format.

Here are some rules to follow:

1. The first line of a paragraph should be indented (縮排) five spaces.

2. Each sentence should start with a capital letter and end with a correct punctuation mark.

3. Each sentence should follow the previous sentence in a logical sequence (順序) until the paragraph is completed.

📖 Example

Write a paragraph by arranging the following statements.

· a waitress came over and brought the elderly lady a clean towel for her wet hair

· the lady noticed that the waitress was heavily pregnant

· she wondered how a person like this waitress could be so thoughtful to a perfect stranger

· the waitress had a sweet smile, one that even being on her feet for an entire day couldn't erase

↓

A waitress came over and brought the elderly lady a clean towel for her wet hair. The waitress had a sweet smile, one that even being on her feet for an entire day couldn't erase. The lady noticed that the waitress was heavily pregnant. She wondered how a person like this waitress could be so thoughtful to a perfect stranger.

Exercise

Arrange the following sentences in a logical sequence and into a paragraph according to the correct format of a paragraph.

1. • a miser hid all of his money in a hole and put a heavy stone to the top
   • he cried so loudly that his neighbors came running to see what was happening
   • one day, he lifted the stone but found no penny there
   • one of the neighbors told him that he didn't need to be unhappy at all
   • since he never thought of how to do with the money

   _____

   _____

   _____

   _____

2. • in Chinese, for example, dogs represent loyalty, and lions are the symbol of authority
   • "as busy as a bee" and "as quiet as a mouse" vividly describe a busy person and a quiet person
   • likewise, animal imagery can be found in many English expressions
   • the imagery gives color to the language
   • in many languages, certain animals have specific characteristics

   _____

   _____

   _____

   _____

   _____

3. • thus, it is common to find pineapples placed in houses during Chinese New Year
   • baozi is another instance
   • no wonder, Chinese people give "baozi" together with "zongzi" to the examinees to wish them a sure victory
   • the pronunciation of the word for "pineapple" in Taiwanese means "prosperity or good luck will come"
   • the word "baozi," together with the word "zongzi," sounds like "a sure victory"
   • naturally, it has become a symbol of wealth in Chinese culture

_____
_____
_____
_____
_____
_____
_____
_____

參考答案請參閱解答本 p. 4

Narrative Writing

15-1 Point of View

Point of view is the perspective from which a story is told. It refers to the position of the person telling the story, namely the narrator, and it tells readers the relationship between the narrator and the other characters. The most common points of view are first-person point of view and third-person point of view.

1. **First-person point of view:** The story is told from the viewpoint of "I," who is often the main or central character in the story. Through the narrator's "first-hand" experience and knowledge, the readers are able to learn what the narrator has been through and know what he or she thinks and how he or she feels.

   Example

   · Jim and **I** got into another fight over the mess he made in the living room again! **I** was trembling with rage after he told **me** to "stop nagging." With his eyes closed, he said that he had been stressed out and needed some silence. **I** stood still next to the sofa and waited for an apology from him. However, **I** almost hit the roof because he just sat there and kept changing channels.

2. **Third-person point of view:** The story is told from the viewpoint of another person. The narrator may not be involved in the story, or he or she may be a supporting character. The narrator usually uses "he," "she," "they," "him," "her," "them," "his," "her," and "their" to tell the story and even reveal the characters' inner thoughts or feelings.

   Example

   · **Joe** was driving **his** battered old car home on a country road one evening. Since the closure of the Levi's factory, **he**'d been unemployed. With winter raging on, the chill had finally hit home.

   It was starting to get dark. Although snow flurries drifted in the dim light of day, **Joe** could still notice **an elderly lady** stranded by the

roadside. Apparently, **she** needed some help. So, **he** pulled up in front of **her** Mercedes-Benz and got out.

Exercise

Read each of the following stories. Write "FN" in the blank if it is a first-person narrative or "TN" if it is a third-person narrative. The first one has been done for you.

TN 1. Harrison's family has been in the ice-cream business for four generations, and Harrison himself has spent almost his whole life in it as well.

_____ 2. Night after night, Mom came to tuck me in, even long after my childhood years. As part of her nightly routine, she would lean down, push my long hair out of the way, and then kiss me on the forehead.

_____ 3. Contrary to Frankenstein's expectations, however, the creature that he had made turned out to be a giant, frightening monster. Frankenstein was so alarmed that he fled in horror. The following day, he returned but found that the monster was gone.

_____ 4. Jack Wang is standing at the gate of his new school.
He is so nervous that his heart is pounding because today is his first day at an American high school.

_____ 5. When I was a kid, I delivered newspapers in my community every day. On a quiet Saturday afternoon, my friend and I were bored, so we randomly picked an old lady's house to be part of our game of throwing stones.

參考答案請參閱解答本 p. 4

15-2 Time Order

When writing a story, we can arrange the events in several different orders. Of these, the most commonly used is "chronological (按時間順序的) order," in which the events are arranged according to the time they occur—the

thing that happens first is told first and then the second thing told second, etc. This kind of structure makes it easy for the readers to understand what happens and when and how the events are connected together. The following are some transitional expressions that you can use to connect the events in chronological order.

first, second, then, next, later, after, before, when, while, meanwhile, finally, eventually, at first, in the meantime, at that moment, as soon as, in the long run, in the end, etc.

📖 Example ▶

On a quiet Saturday afternoon, my friends and I threw rocks onto an old lady's roof out of boredom. Unfortunately, I accidentally broke a window **as** the stone slipped out of my hand.

For the next few days, I was so worried about myself that I did not think of the old lady and her broken window. **Later on, when** I was sure that I wasn't in trouble, I started to feel guilty. Every day, the old lady greeted me with a warm smile **as** I passed her the newspaper, but I didn't feel comfortable in her presence anymore.

Finally, I made up my mind to save the money which I made from delivering newspapers. **In three weeks**, I had enough money to repair her window. I put the money in an envelope and wrote a note that said, "I am sorry for breaking your window. I hope that the money will cover the cost of repairing it."

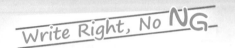

**Exercise**

Arrange the following events (A-I) in chronological order and then circle the transitional expressions that represent time.

○ ○ ○ ○ ○ ○ ○ ○ ○ ○ ○ ○ ○ ○ ○ ○ ○ ○

A. Finally, the spirit got a chance to explain. It complained that the Thao were blinded by their greed and were emptying the lake of its fish.

B. Numa then told the tribe's elders what had happened in the lake.

C. One day, a group of Thao fishermen found that their fishing nets had been seriously damaged, but no one knew the reason for this.

D. To avoid catching baby fish, the Thao no longer used small-mesh nets from then on.

E. After he jumped into the water, he headed directly for its deepest area and came upon the answer there—a long-haired spirit was destroying the Thao's fishing nets.

F. He made peace with the long-haired spirit before he returned to his tribe.

G. Numa, a strong Thao hero, volunteered to go into the lake to find out the cause of it.

H. When Numa heard what the spirit said, he was shocked and embarrassed. It dawned on him that the lake had supported his tribe for generations.

I. Numa swam quickly toward it and tried to stop it from tearing more of the nets. The two then had a fierce fight underwater for three days.

The correct order is _____ → _____ → _____ → _____ → _____ → _____ → _____ → _____ → _____ .

參考答案請參閱解答本 p. 4

15-3 Writing a Narrative Paragraph

Narrative writing (敘述寫作) tells a story with supporting details, describes an event or experience, or makes a point by explaining what has happened in a certain situation. Supporting details need to be presented and arranged in a specific order so that readers will have no trouble understanding the information. The following are some tips on how to write an effective narrative paragraph.

1. Brainstorm

Write down as many ideas related to the topic as you can. Cross out any ideas that are not directly related to your topic, and group the relevant ones together.

2. Write a Rough Outline

Think of a topic sentence that best describes the idea you want to express in the paragraph, and then organize the supporting ideas in chronological order.

Example

Topic: Watching a Horror Movie

1. Brainstorm

1. dead people came alive and turned into zombies
2. zombies look no different from living people
3. frightened by the bloody scenes
4. turned the volume up
5. turned off the TV
6. headed back to my room
7. scared to death and nearly passed out
8. the darkness of the room made it creepier
9. heard footsteps behind me and a voice whispering my name
10. my heart pounded wildly
11. the ghost-like figure was my mom

Group A:
1. dead people came alive and turned into zombies
3. frightened by the bloody scenes
8. the darkness of the room made it creepier

Group B:
5. turned off the TV
6. headed back to my room

Group C:
7. scared to death and nearly passed out
9. heard footsteps behind me and a voice whispering my name
10. my heart pounded wildly
11. the ghost-like figure was my mom

2. Write a Rough Outline

The Topic Sentence: Last Friday night, I watched a horror movie alone at home.

The Supporting Ideas: ① Group A: became scared
② Group B: decided to stop watching
③ Group C: frightened by a ghost-like figure and then discovered who it really was

3. Write a Paragraph

The topic sentence (1)

The supporting sentences (2~12)

¹Last Friday night, I watched a horror movie alone at home. ²[At first, I did not think it would be too scary, so I turned off the light and lay down on the sofa to watch the film by myself. ³However, right after the movie started, I found out that I was wrong—it was really scary. ⁴I was really terrified when dead people started turning into zombies and coming back to life. ⁵As blood splattered everywhere on the TV screen, the darkness in the room made it even creepier. ⁶Finally, I decided to turn off the TV. ⁷Just as I was about to head back to my room, I heard footsteps behind me and a voice whispering my name. ⁸I tried to tell myself that it was only my imagination, but the voice kept coming back. ⁹My heart pounded wildly, and I was very afraid. ¹⁰It was not my imagination! ¹¹There really was someone behind the sofa! ¹²At the moment I was just about to pass out, that "someone" turned the

The concluding sentence (13)

light on.] ¹³[To my great relief, it was my mom, saying that she had heard some noise in the living room.]

Exercise

Write a narrative paragraph according to the following topic. Brainstorm first, and then prepare a rough outline for your paragraph. Develop your ideas into complete sentences, and then organize them into a paragraph. Finally, bring the paragraph to an end with a good concluding sentence.

Topic: A Bad Day in My Life

1. Brainstorm

2. Write a Rough Outline

The Topic Sentence: _____

The Supporting Ideas: _____

_____

_____

3. Write a Paragraph

_____

_____

_____

_____

_____

_____

参考答案請參閱解答本 p. 4～5

Unit 16

Picture Writing

Picture writing is mostly about narrative writing: telling a story. This story must be closely connected with a person or an event. Vivid details are an important part of the story. A reasonable, convincing or outstanding ending makes the story attractive. There are two types of picture description tasks: One is writing about a single image, and the other involves writing about multiple images, usually a series of three or four.

16-1 Picture writing about a single image

Below are the steps toward writing an effective single-picture essay.

1. **Read the picture**

   Look at the picture carefully. What is the picture about? First, decide whether the picture will serve as the beginning, the middle, or the conclusion of a narrative. Then, decide on the main idea or key point you want to write about. Lastly, create the supporting details to make the story complete.

2. **Set up the scene and characters**

   The story can be told from different points of view. However, it will be easier to tell a story from the first-person perspective or give the main character a name. Decide where and when a story takes place.

3. **Give supporting details**

   Think of how you would like the story to go on. Since there is only one picture, there is much room for thought. You can exercise your imagination and creativity to create a story you wish. You should consider the situation, motivation, or process that leads to the conclusion you have made. Be sure to make your story logical and persuasive. It is important to involve a key point or main idea you want to convey.

The following are the organization and the tips for picture writing.

- Like all the writing, picture writing should include three parts: the introduction, the body (the plot or the details of what has happened), and the conclusion.

- In addition to telling the events of the story, you should also pay attention to the structure, the accuracy of sentences, proper wording (措辭) and fluency.

- Writing about pictures is a form of narrative writing, That is, it is usually about something happening in the past. Therefore, a past tense is used to tell the story.

- Don't ever try to use difficult wording or complicated structures you are not familiar with. After all, getting the meaning across is the most important thing, not showing off your skills.

 Example

Look at the following picture and write a paragraph based on the picture.

Before writing

1. Read the picture:
   - The man feels sorry.
   - The woman is angry.
   - It's a story about lovers.
2. Set up the scene and characters:
   - A man and a woman.
   - They are lovers.
   - They are at a restaurant.
3. Give supporting details:
   - Why is the woman angry?
   - What does the man do?
   - What is the result?

Write a Paragraph

　　Mary had a date with her boyfriend last Saturday evening. They planned to have a romantic dinner and then see a romantic movie. Mary was all dressed up, and she arrived at the appointed place on time. She was excited and couldn't wait to see her boyfriend. After half an hour had passed, Mary was impatient because her boyfriend didn't show up. When her boyfriend finally showed up, Mary had been waiting for fifty minutes. Mary lost her temper in spite of his apology. Suddenly, he took out a ring from his pocket and kneeled down—and proposed to her. He promised her that he would not let her wait again. She was so surprised that she forgot about her anger, and she agreed to become his wife. Well, this is the story my mother repeatedly told me about how my father proposed to her.

Exercise

Look at the picture below and write a story based on the picture. Your paragraph should be at least 120 words in length.

參考答案請參閱解答本 p. 5

16-2 Picture writing about multiple images

This type of picture writing always consists of a series of three or four pictures. It may depict (描繪) a clearly closed ending or leave the ending open to interpretation.

Below are the steps toward writing about pictures with a closed ending.

1. **Read the pictures**

   Look at the pictures carefully. What is each picture about? Look at the first and last picture again and decide what happens in the beginning and at the conclusion of the story.

2. **Set up the scene and characters**

   You may describe it as your own story, or a story of your friend, your relative or someone you know. You may also name the characters and decide on the place and the time the story takes place.

3. **Give supporting details**

   In multiple-image picture writing, the conclusion is basically given to you; therefore, it's the plot that makes a difference. Think of how you would like the story to go on. What is the situation, motivation and process? What is the key point or main idea you want to convey to the readers? Be sure to connect the pictures logically, originally, and dramatically if possible.

📖 Example

Look at the following pictures and write a complete story based on the pictures. Your story should be at least 120 words in length.

①  ②

Before writing

1. Read each picture: (1) The woman is waiting at a restaurant, looking happy.

(2) The man is coming. The woman looks angry.

(3) The man is giving a bouquet of flowers to the woman. The woman still has a look of unhappiness.

(4) The man is kneeling down, showing a ring. The woman is smiling to him.

2. Set up the scene and characters: (1) They are lovers.

(2) It is a day for proposal.

3. Give supporting details: (1) What happened on that day?

(2) How did the man do to win the love?

(3) Why did the woman forgive the man?

Write a Paragraph

　　Serena had been in a relationship with her boyfriend for more than two years. They had a date to have dinner in a new restaurant downtown and see a romantic movie afterwards. Wearing her best outfit, Serena arrived at the meeting place on time. She was excited and couldn't wait to see her boyfriend. Ten minutes passed, but Serena's boyfriend didn't show up. "The traffic must be busy," she thought. After she had waited twenty minutes, Serena began to get worried, afraid something might have happened. Half an hour passed, Serena now was simply impatient. When her boyfriend finally arrived, he was forty minutes late. He apologized over and over again, but she paid no attention to him. He handed her the flowers he had gotten for her, but she refused. She criticized him for all the times he had been late in the past two years and burst into tears. Suddenly, he took out a ring from his pocket, kneeled down and proposed to her. He promised her that he would not let her wait again. This made her cry even louder. This is the story my mother repeatedly told me of how she agreed to marry my father.

Below are the steps toward writing about pictures with an open ending.

1. Like pictures with a closed ending, the plot is there. Therefore, read pictures, try to find the link between the pictures and make up a story about how everything is going on just as you do with a closed ending.

2. Unlike writing pictures with a closed ending, the writer holds the key to the ending. Therefore, the writer may choose to lead either a happy or a sad ending. Be sure to end the story following the previous happenings so that the story is logical and appealing.

📖 Example ▶

Look at the following pictures and write a complete story based on the pictures. Your story should be at least 120 words in length.

①  ②

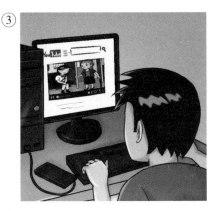 

Before writing

1. Read each picture: (1) A high school girl was sitting with her eyes closed in one of the priority seats on the MRT. An elderly woman is standing next to her.

(2) A passenger videotaped the scene.

(3) The passenger posted the video on YouTube.

2. Set up the scene and characters: (1) It was on the MRT.

(2) It was something about the priority seats.

(3) A high school girl, an elderly woman, and some passengers.

3. Give supporting details: (1) What did the high school girl do?

(2) What happened to the elderly woman?

(3) What did the other passengers on the MRT do?

(4) What might happen after the man post the video on YouTube?

Write a Paragraph

A high school girl was sitting with her eyes closed in one of the priority seats on the MRT. She was apparently unaware of an elderly woman standing right beside her. Without the high school girl's knowledge, a passenger had videotaped the scene and posted it on YouTube. Before long, the clip had gotten tens of thousands of views, and hundreds of messages were posted, most of which were savage words. They criticized the girl for keeping the seat by pretending to be sleeping. They even found out the girl's identity with "human flesh search engines." Numerous malicious messages were posted on her Facebook page. At this point, one of the girl's teachers spoke up for her. He said the student had had a terrible stomachache that day and had every right to sit on the priority seat. As a result of this incident, people began to realize the "unseen" needs of some passengers. So, I learn a lesson: We should never make a hasty judgment until we know the whole story.

Exercise

Look at the following pictures and write a complete story based on the pictures. Your story should be at least 120 words in length.

①

②

③

④

參考答案請參閱解答本 p. 5～6

Unit 17

Descriptive Writing

17-1 Describing a Person

A descriptive paragraph creates a "word picture" of someone or something, and it allows readers to "see" the picture. When you describe a person, make sure you provide plenty of details so that readers can create a picture in their own minds that calls on the five senses (sight, hearing, smell, taste, and touch).

The following are the steps in writing a descriptive paragraph.

1. Brainstorm

Use your imagination and list as many ideas as you can. After writing down these ideas, organize the details you have come up with. Cross out any ideas that are not directly related to your topic, and group the relevant ones together.

2. Write a Rough Outline

Think of a topic sentence that best describes the idea you want to express in the paragraph, and then organize and put the supporting ideas in logic sequence.

Adjectives that are often used when you are describing a person can be categorized as follows:

1. Physical appearance:

> fit, well-built, brown-eyed, good-looking, handsome, attractive, pretty, ordinary, plain, overweight, pale, etc.

2. Positive personality:

> trustworthy, confident, clever, easy-going, humorous, generous, energetic, honest, thoughtful, patient, etc.

3. Negative personality:

> mean, irresponsible, selfish, lazy, big-headed, cowardly, boring, careless, cruel, jealous, etc.

 **Example**

Topic: My Father

1. Brainstorm

1. tall and fit
2. simple short hair cut
3. looks young
4. ~~takes exercise twice a week~~
5. handsome
6. in his mid forties
7. thoughtful and sympathetic
8. hard-working and diligent
9. takes good care of the family
10. does volunteer work

Group A:
1. tall and fit
2. simple short hair cut
3. looks young
5. handsome
6. in his mid forties

Group B:
7. thoughtful and sympathetic
8. hard-working and diligent

Group C:
9. takes good care of the family
10. does volunteer work

2. Write a Rough Outline

The Topic Sentence: My father is a very special man in many ways.

The Supporting Ideas: ① Group A: his looks
                ② Group B: his personality
                ③ Group C: his good behavior

3. Write a Paragraph

The topic sentence (1)

The supporting sentences (2~9)

[1]My father is a very special man in many ways. [2][He has simple short hair cut. [3]Tall and fit, he often wears jeans when he goes out. [4]Because he looks so young and handsome, he is often mistaken for my elder brother, even though he is now in his mid-forties. [5]Having grown up in a poor family makes my father cherish what he has now. [6]So, he works hard to make sure we have a better home environment than he did. [7]As a busy father who has his own job, he not only

does his job very well, but also helps to take good care of his family all the time. [8]What's more, he is very thoughtful and sympathetic, and he does volunteer work to help people in need. [9]He believes that it is more blessed to give than to receive.] [10][To me, he is a role model as well as my father, and it's just great to have an excellent father like him.]

The concluding sentence (10)

Exercise

Now it's your turn to write a descriptive paragraph. Brainstorm first, and then prepare a rough outline for your paragraph. Develop your ideas into complete sentences, and then organize them into a paragraph. Finally, bring the paragraph to an end with a good concluding sentence.

Topic: My Best Friend

1. Brainstorm

2. Write a Rough Outline

The Topic Sentence: _____

The Supporting Ideas: _____

_____

3. Write a Paragraph

參考答案請參閱解答本 p. 6

17-2 Describing a Place

When you describe a place, first you have to tell the readers where the place is and then give a brief description of it. When organizing the supporting details, you may mention special natural features or other special local sites. In your conclusion, you can tell the readers how you feel about the place or why you want them to know about it.

The following steps can help you write an effective descriptive paragraph about a place.

1. Brainstorm

List as many details of the place as possible. Cross out any irrelevant ideas, and group the relevant ones together. Also, follow a logical order, such as from left to right, top to down, outside to inside, or clockwise (順時針地), etc. To come up with more ideas, you may also ask yourself the following questions:

· Where is the place? What does the place look like? What happens in the place?

· What do I think of the place? What does the place mean to me?

2. Write a Rough Outline

Think of a topic sentence that best describes the idea you want to express in the paragraph, and then organize and put the supporting ideas in logic sequence.

📖 Example

Topic: Neiwan—A Village of White Tung Blossoms

1. Brainstorm

1. an attractive Hakka village
2. most villagers used to earn their living cutting down trees or farming
3. it costs about NT$20 to go from Zhudong to Neiwan by train
4. in the Zhudong area, the eastern part of Hsinchu County
5. Hakka is not easy to learn
6. coal was mined there
7. the government decided to restore Neiwan
8. White Tung Blossoms Festival
9. Hakka pounded tea and wild ginger flower flavored rice dumplings
10. Neiwan Theater

Group A:
1. an attractive Hakka village
4. in the Zhudong area, the eastern part of Hsinchu County

Group B:
2. most villagers used to earn their living cutting down trees or farming
6. coal was mined there
7. the government decided to restore Neiwan

Group C:
8. White Tung Blossoms Festival
9. Hakka pounded tea and wild ginger flower flavored rice dumplings
10. Neiwan Theater

2. Write a Rough Outline

The Topic Sentence: Neiwan is an attractive Hakka village.

The Supporting Ideas: ① Group A: location
② Group B: local history
③ Group C: tourist attractions and local specialties

3. Write a Paragraph

The topic sentence (1) >

¹Neiwan is an attractive Hakka village in the Zhudong area, the eastern part of Hsinchu County.

The supporting sentences (2~10) >

²[During the Japanese colonial era, most villagers there used to earn their living by cutting down trees or farming. ³Later, coal was mined there, and Neiwan soon became a prosperous coal mining area. ⁴However, because of restrictions on mining, Neiwan lost its economic importance and the population also dropped. ⁵In 2000, the government started a project to restore Neiwan to its former glory. ⁶With the efforts of both government officials and local residents, Neiwan has since become a very popular tourist spot. ⁷Every April and May, visitors to this attractive village can appreciate the natural beauty of the Tung blossoms. ⁸In addition, Neiwan is famous for Hakka snacks, particularly Hakka pounded tea and wild ginger flower flavored rice dumplings. ⁹Last but not least, the Neiwan theater is definitely worth visiting. ¹⁰Built in the 1950s, it has now been turned into a restaurant in which visitors can watch old movies as they enjoy a

The concluding sentence (11) >

meal there.] ¹¹[Next time, if you want to take a one-day trip, Neiwan might be a good choice—it will take your breath away.]

**Exercise**

Now it's your turn to write a descriptive paragraph.

Topic: The Most Unforgettable Place I Have Visited

1. Brainstorm

2. Write a Rough Outline

The Topic Sentence: _____

_____

The Supporting Ideas: _____

_____

_____

3. Write a Paragraph

_____

_____

_____

_____

_____

_____

_____

_____

_____

_____

_____

_____

_____

_____

_____

_____

_____

參考答案請參閱解答本 p. 6～7

17-3 Describing an Object

When you describe an object, you should try to make your readers feel what you feel and see what you see. That is, a good description can help readers clearly imagine the object.

The following are tips for writing a good paragraph to describe an object.

1. Choose an object that you have strong feelings about. It should be something you either like or dislike very much.

2. Start with your general impression of the object when you start writing the main idea.

3. Make use of the five senses to describe the object. For example, you can ask yourself "what does it look, sound, smell, taste, or feel like?"

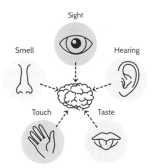

4. Use some adjectives to describe the object. If you use more than one adjective, the order should be as follows: number→opinion→size→shape→color→origin →material→purpose.

5. Follow a logical order, such as from left to right, top to down, outside to inside, or clockwise, etc.

6. Describe your strongest impression last.

7. State your main idea again to conclude your paragraph.

📖 Example

Topic: The Most Valuable Thing I Have

1. Brainstorm

1. battered brown leather band
2. silver case
3. the first watch that I received from my parents
4. neither water nor scratch resistant
5. a gift for my tenth birthday
6. Mickey Mouse on the face
7. special hour and minute hands
8. date function
9. battery-operated
10. used for seven years

Group A:
1. battered brown leather band
2. silver case
6. Mickey Mouse on the face
7. special hour and minute hands

Group B:
4. neither water nor scratch resistant
8. date function
9. battery-operated

Group C:
3. the first watch that I received from my parents
5. a gift for my tenth birthday
10. used for seven years

2. Write a Rough Outline

The Topic Sentence: The most valuable thing I have is an old automatic watch

The Supporting Ideas: ① Group A: its appearance
② Group B: its function
③ Group C: its value

3. Write a Paragraph

The topic sentence (1)

The supporting sentences (2~6)

[1]The most valuable thing I have is an old automatic watch with a battered brown leather band—the first watch that I received from my parents as a gift for my tenth birthday. [2][The watch has a silver case and features Mickey Mouse in full color on its white face.

[3]The cutest thing is that his little arms act as the hour and minute hands. [4]The date function is located at the 3:00 spot. [5]It is battery-operated. [6]Though it's not Swiss made, not licensed by Disney, and not even water or scratch resistant, it is the watch that has been keeping me company and telling me the time for the past seven years.] [7][Bought at a stand at a night market, the cartoon watch was not expensive at all, but it is the thing that I cherish most.]

> The concluding sentence (7)

Exercise

Now it's your turn to write a descriptive paragraph.

Topic: My School Uniform

1. Brainstorm

2. Write a Rough Outline

The Topic Sentence: _____

_____

The Supporting Ideas: _____

_____

_____

3. Write a Paragraph

参考答案請參閱解答本 p. 7～8

Unit 18

Letter Writing

18-1 Formats of Letters

I. Formal letter writing

Formal letters are written for business, application for a job, admission to a college and to an institution, or for something related to a company or institution.

The following are what formal letter writing should include:

1. **Heading**: The sender's address. It is written at the top of the letter.

2. **Date**: Do not abbreviate the month.

3. **Inside address**: It contains the name, title, and complete address of the person you are sending your letter to.

4. **Salutation** (稱謂語): In a formal letter, salutation is followed by a colon. The most commonly used salutations are as follows:

   (1) Dear Mr. (last name), Dear Ms. (last name), Dear Mrs. (last name), Dear Miss (last name)

   (2) If you are not sure who might read your letter, use "Dear Sir" "Dear Madam" "Dear Sir or Madam" "Dear Sirs" or "To Whom It May Concern"

5. **Body**: The message of the letter should be clearly stated. The content should be concise and to the point. Wording should be formal.

6. **Complimentary close** (結尾敬語): It is always followed by a comma, not a period. Some commonly used complimentary closes in formal letters are: "Yours respectfully," "Respectfully," "Sincerely yours," "Yours sincerely," "Sincerely," "Yours truly," "Truly yours," "Best regards," etc.

7. **Signature**: It contains two parts: the handwritten signature and the typed signature.

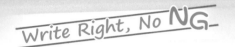

There are primary three forms of letter writing, including full-block form (齊頭式), modified-block form (改良齊平式), and semi-block/indented form (半齊頭式). Below are the formats of each form.

1. **full-block form**

   Heading, date, inside address, greeting, salutation, body of the letter, complimentary close, and signature are written or typed flush (對齊的) with the left margin (頁邊). Skipping a line between paragraphs is more formal. This is considered the most formal formats and most commonly used because it is thought convenient and time saving.

(heading)
(date)
(inside address)
(greeting/salutation):
(body of the letter)
XXXXXXXXXXXXXXXXXXXXXXXXXXXXXXXXXXXXXXXXXXXXXXXXXXX XXXXXXXXXXXXXXXXXXXXXXXXXXXXXXXXXXXXXXXXXXXXXXXXXX XXXXXXXXXXXXXXXXXXXXXXXXXXXX.
(complimentary close),
(handwritten signature)
(typed signature)

2. **modified-block form**

   Date, heading, complimentary close, and signature are placed in the middle. The body of the letter and the other parts of the letter are placed flush with the left. It depends whether to skip a line between paragraphs or not. This form is becoming widely accepted.

(heading)

(date)

(inside address)

(salutation):

(body of the letter)
XXXXXXXXXXXXXXXXXXXXXXXXXXXXXXXXXXXXXXXXXXXXXXXXXXXX
XXXXXXXXXXXXXXXXXXXXXXXXXXXXXXXXXXXXXXXXXXXXXXXXXXXX
XXXXXXXXXXXXXXXXXXXXXXXXXXXXXXXX.

(complimentary close),

(handwritten signature)
(typed signature)

---

3. **semi-block/indented form**

Date, heading, complimentary close, and signature are placed in the middle. The other parts including the recipient's name and address, salutation and greeting are placed flush with the left like those of the block form. Each paragraph of the body of the letter is indented with five spaces from the left margin. Skipping a line between paragraphs is preferable. This is the form commonly used in hand-written letters.

(heading)

(date)

(inside address)

(salutation):

(body of the letter)

XXXXXXXXXXXXXXXXXXXXXXXXXXXXXXXXXXXXXXXXXXXXXXX
XXXXXXXXXXXXXXXXXXXXXXXXXXXXXXXXXXXXXXXXXXXXXXX
XXXXXXXXXXXXXXXXXXXXXXXXXXXXXX.

(complimentary close),

(handwritten signature)
(typed signature)

📖 Example ▶

The following is a format of a job application letter sent by Susan Lin to the World Trading Company.

8F., No. 100, Sec. 3, Datong Rd.,
Neipu Township, Pingtung County 91244 } *heading*

May 10, 2016 ←*date*

Mr. Marley
General Manager
World Trading Company
10F., No. 258, Sec. 2, Bade Rd.,
Zhongshan Dist., Taipei City 10492 } *inside address*

Dear Mr. Marley: ←*salutation*
XXXXXXXXXXXXXXXXXXXXXXXXXXXXXXXXXXXXXXXXXXXXXXXXXX
XXXXXXXXXXXXXXXXXXXXXXXXXXXXXXXXXXXXXXXXXXXXXXXXXX
XXXXXXXXXXXXXXXXXXXXXXXXXXXXXX.

XXXXXXXXXXXXXXXXXXXXXXXXXXXXXXXXXXXXXXXXXXXXXXXXXX

XXXXXXXXXXXXXXXXXXXXXXXXXXXXXXXXXXXXXXXXXXXXXXXX
XXXXX.

Sincerely, ←*complimentary close*

Susan Lin ←*handwritten signature*
Susan Lin ←*typed signature*

II. Informal letter writing

Informal or personal letters are often used to express one's appreciation, regret, concern, needs, or feelings. They can also be used to inform someone of something or invite someone to an event.

Differences between informal and formal letter writing are as follows:

1. **Heading and inside address**: These two parts are often omitted (刪除).

2. **Date**: Write down the date in the middle.

3. **Salutation**: This usually begins with the word "Dear" followed by the first name of the person who you are sending

> (date)
> (salutation),
> (body of the letter)
>
> (complimentary close),
> (signature)

   your letter to, and it is followed by a comma, e.g. "Dear (first name)," "Dear friend," or "My dear friend," "Hello/Hi (first name)" can also be used. If the letter is addressed to a family member, the name may be replaced with family relationship such as "Dear brother" or "Dear Mom."

4. **Body**: This contains the message that you wish to communicate. Wording is less formal or even very informal, based on your relationship with the person you are writing to. You can indent the first sentence of each paragraph.

5. **Complimentary close**: Complimentary close is placed either in the middle or flush to the left. Some commonly used complimentary closes in informal letters are: "Love," "Best wishes," "Regards," "Your loving daughter," "Dad," etc.

6. **Signature**: A typed signature is not necessary. Write your first name below the complimentary close.

📖 **Example**

The following is a letter sent by Susan to her friend Andrew.

> Oct. 20, 2016 ←*date*
>
> Dear Andrew, ←*salutation*
>
> XXXXXXXXXXXXXXXXXXXXXXXXXXXXXXXXXXXXXXXXXXXXXXXXXXXX
> XXXXXXXXXXXXXXXXXXXXXXXXXXXXXXXXXXXXXXXXXXXXXXXXXXXX
> XXXXXXXXXXXXXXXXXXXXXXXXXX.
>
> Best wishes, ←*complimentary close*
>
> Susan ←*handwritten signature*

III. Addressing the envelope

🔍 The following are some rules for addressing the envelope.

1. Put your name and address in the top left-hand corner. The address is usually divided into two or three lines.

2. Skip two lines from the sender's address. Place the name and address of the recipient in the middle of the envelop.

3. The stamp is placed in the top right-hand corner.

4. When writing the postal address, start with Floor, then Number, Alley, Lane, Street or Road, County, City, Country, and Zip Code comes last.

Chinese-English glossary of the Chinese address

樓 Floor (F.)	號 Number (No.)	巷 Lane (Ln.)
弄 Alley (Aly.)	街 Street (St.)	路 Road (Rd.)
大道 Boulevard (Blvd.)	大街 Avenue (Ave.)	段 Section (Sec.)
村 Village	鄉 Township	鎮 Town
區 District (Dist.)	縣 County	市 City

 **Example**

Below is the envelope of a letter sent by Susan to her friend Andrew.

Susan Lin
8F., No. 100, Sec. 3, Datong Rd.,
Neipu Township, Pingtung County 91244 *the sender's address*

the recipient's address
Mr. Andrew Wang
6F., No. 50, Ln. 42, Minxiang St.,
Yonghe District, New Taipei City 23454

 **Exercise A**

Fill in each of the blanks below with at least three proper salutations and complimentary closes.

	Salutation	**Complimentary close**
Formal letters		
Informal letters		

參考答案請參閱解答本 p. 8

Exercise B

Complete the format of a formal letter addressed to a university or a company. (Be sure to include everything needed for a formal letter such as heading, date, inside address, complimentary close and signature.) Use "X" for the body of the letter.

_____

_____

_____

_____

_____

_____

XXXXXXXXXXXXXXXXXXXXXXXXXXXXXXXXXXXXXXXXXXXXXXXXX
XXXXXXXXXXXXXXXXXXXXXXXXXXXXXXXXXXXXXXXXXXXXXXXXX
XXXXXXXXXXXXXXXXXXXXXXXXXXXXXXXXXXXXXX.

XXXXXXXXXXXXXXXXXXXXXXXXXXXXXXXXXXXXXXXXXXXXXXXXX
XXXXXXXXXXXXXXXXXXXXXXXXXXXXXXXXXXXXXXXXXXXXXXXXX
XXXXXXXXXXXXXXXXXXXXXXXXXXXXXXXXXXXXXX.

_____

_____

參考答案請參閱解答本 p. 8

Exercise C

Complete the format of the letter to your friend Lily Wang. (Be sure to include everything needed for a personal letter. Use "X" for the body of the letter.)

_____

_____

XXXXXXXXXXXXXXXXXXXXXXXXXXXXXXXXXXXXXXXXXXXXXXXXX
XXXXXXXXXXXXXXXXXXXXXXXXXXXXXXXXXXXXXXXXXXXXXXXXX
XXXXXXXXXXXXXXXXXXXXXXXXXXXXXXXXXXXX.

_____

_____

参考答案請參閱解答本 p. 8

Exercise D

Address the envelope below to a university or company. Use your own address for the return address.

_____

_____

_____

_____

_____

_____

_____

参考答案請參閱解答本 p. 8

18-2 Types of Letter Writing

I. Request Letters

Request letters are usually written to ask for information, advice, services, etc. They are widely used in our daily lives. For instance, when a computer store cannot refund (退款) the money you have paid for a broken item, you may have to write a request letter to the manufacturer and ask for a refund.

The following are some rules of a request letter.

1. Always make sure that the letter is brief and to the point.

2. Clearly state the problem and politely state your request(s).

3. Express your appreciation to the person who will receive and deal with your request.

4. Provide your contact information, such as your (e-mail) address or your phone number.

📖 Example ▶

The following is a request letter to ask the computer store to refund the money Susan has paid for a damaged computer.

11F., No. 18, Fuyi Rd.,
Taiping Dist., Taichung City 41158

March 30, 2016

General Manager
Apple Inc.
19F. A, No. 1, Songzhi Rd.,
Xinyi Dist., Taipei City 11047

Dear Sir or Madam,

On March 14, I bought a computer in one of your agencies at No. 68, Gongyi Rd., Taichung City. I paid NT$35,000 for a brand-new MacBook Pro, as shown on the enclosed copy of the sales slip. (←*background*)

It worked well for a week, but it suddenly crashed while I was using it on March 22. After that, I couldn't boot it up anymore. I immediately contacted the agency where I had bought the computer, but the clerk refused to refund the money I had paid for this computer. (←*state the problem*)

However, as far as I know, Apple Inc. always has the one-year refund policy. I think your company should take responsibility for this situation and give me a full refund for this damaged computer. I would appreciate it if you could write or call me at (04)1233-2312 at your earliest convenience. Thank you for your assistance. (←*propose a solution and provide contact information*)

Sincerely,
Susan Lin
Susan Lin

Exercise

Based on the given information below, write a request letter to Twinkle Department Store.

Sender's address: No. 28, Xinzhan Rd., Banqiao Dist., New Taipei City 22041

Sender's name: Jane Wang

Date: May 5, 2016

Recipient's title: Sales Manager

Recipient's address: No. 386, Fushing North Rd., Zhongshan Dist., Taipei City 10476

_____

_____

_____

_____

_____

_____

_____

_____

_____

_____

_____

_____

參考答案請參閱解答本 p. 8～9

II. Application Letters

Application letters are the letters for applying for a job or for admission to a college. Such letters must include your education background, experience and interest and focus on how or why you are qualified and competent.

In general, there are four paragraphs.

1st paragraph: Briefly explain the reason(s) and motivation for applying for the job or the department. In applying for a job, you may also explain how you get the information.

2nd paragraph: Focus on your interest and qualification. Provide specific proof and performance, if there is any.

3rd paragraph: What and how will you do if you <u>are admitted to the school/get the job</u>? What is your future plan?

Closing: Express your eagerness for the opportunity.

📖 Example A ➡

The following is an application letter for admission to a college.

No. 264, Chung-hwa Rd.,
East Dist., Hsinchu 30020

May 5, 2016

English Department
National Taiwan Normal University
162, Section 1, Heping E. Rd.,
Taipei City 106

Dear Sirs or Madams,

I am writing for the admission to the English Department. I have been interested in English since I entered junior high. Your school has been my first choice because of its excellent reputation and because of the outstanding performance of the graduates. (*←state the motivation for applying*)

I spend lots of time on English. Besides the textbooks, I like reading English magazines and novels. Sometimes I will listen to ICRT and watch CNN to enlarge my vocabulary and improve my listening ability. I not only score high on English tests but I also won the first prize in the speech contest. Besides, I am the chairperson of the English conversation club in my school. The more I get involved in English, the more determined I am to choose English as my major. My sister graduated from your department and now is studying in the States. I think she has influenced me a lot. I would follow her example. (*←qualifications*)

After graduation from the English Department, I'll go on with further studies in English literature. I have confidence in myself. I do hope I have the opportunity to be admitted and I am sure to study with enthusiasm. (←*future plan*)

I have included letters of recommendation, my autobiography, transcript, and certificates of merit for English shows and speech contest. I am looking forward to hearing from you soon. (←*closing with inference to enclosed documents*)

Sincerely yours,
May Chang
May Chang

📖 Example B ▶

The following is an application letter for applying for a job.

No. 160, Sec. 2, Ging-Ko Rd.,
North Dist., Hsinchu 300

October 5, 2016

Bank of Taiwan
No. 120, Sec. 1, Chongqing S. Rd.,
Taipei City 10007, Taiwan

Dear Sirs or Madams,

I am writing for applying for the position of Bank teller advertised in Liberty Daily News. Whatever the result, I am excited to have the opportunity to give it a try. After all, Bank of Taiwan has perfect system and reputation and I am sure that not only can I put what I have learned into practice but I can learn more. (←*state the motivation for applying*)

I graduated from the Department of Finance and Banking, Taiwan University and worked for a Business company for almost one year. Besides learning from the books, I worked as a trainee in another bank during summer vacation when I was a sophomore and junior. Having access to banking business, I am sure that I have made the right decision. I am also sure that I have been interested in my major and I will be competent. (←*qualifications*)

Finance plays an important role not only in business but in the government. The world has been changing fast these years. I think financial management will be more influential and will be dealt with in different ways. I'll work, learn and probably go on further studies. I have confidence in myself. I do hope I have the opportunity. (←*future plan*)

As requested, I am enclosing my transcript and resume. I am looking forward to hearing from you soon. (←*closing with inference to enclosed documents*)

Sincerely yours,
Henry Chang
Henry Chang

III. Invitation Letters

An invitation letter can be either formal or informal. Whether it is formal or informal, be sure to provide enough information so that the receiver will make a decision on whether or not to attend a planned event or join an organization.

The following are some elements that an invitation letter has to include:

1. **what**: the purpose, the food served, the dress code, etc.
2. **who**: the person who invites and who will be invited
3. **when**: the time to hold it and the time to reply to the letter
4. **where**: the place to hold it

5. **how**: how to conduct the activity and how to make connection

6. **RSVP**: meaning "please reply"

7. Other information required

Some tips for writing an invitation letter:

1. A formal invitation can begin with "(the name of the host) request the honor of your presence for (the event)." An invitation card begins with "You are cordially invited to (the event)."

2. Use appropriate tone in the letters, depending on the relationship between you and the receiver. For example, if it is a personal party or you know the receiver well, you can use a more casual tone. If it is a formal party held by a company, wording should be more formal.

3. It is best to keep letters as short and concise as possible.

4. State how eagerly you are looking forward to seeing your guests.

5. Provide your contact information such as your (e-mail) address or phone number.

📖 Example A

The following is a formal invitation card to the graduation party.

> You are cordially invited to my graduation party
>
> Who: Every member of Class 308
>
> When: July 30th, 2016, 6:30 p.m.
>
> Where: Happy KTV (No. 150, Xin 1st Rd. Xinyi Dist., Keelung City)
>
> Why: To celebrate the graduation
>
> What: Singing and celebrating with food and drink supplied by the KTV
>
> RSVP by July 23, 2016, to Paul at 0988-000-000.
>
> The attendees have to prepare a small gift.
>
> At the end of the party is the gift-giving by drawing lots.

 **Example B**

The following is an informal invitation letter to the graduation party.

> July 14, 2016
>
> Dear Mary,
>
> I would like to welcome you to my graduation party at my home at 6:30 p.m., July 30.
>
> We will soon go to different colleges. I think we should meet and have fun before we say goodbye. I do hope we will be close friends forever. So, I plan to invite everyone in our class.
>
> Please reply before July 23 through e-mail or phone call because I will need to prepare some party foods. By the way, please prepare a gift so that we can exchange the gifts at the end of the party. Hope to see you.
>
> Your friend,
>
> Paul

Exercise

Write a formal invitation card for the reunion of your junior high school: Class 314 of 2015.

> _____
>
> Who: _____
>
> When: _____
>
> Where: _____
>
> Why: _____
>
> _____
>
> _____

參考答案請參閱解答本 p. 9

IV. Apology Letters

Letters of apology are written to say that you are sorry and to ask for forgiveness. There are times when you hurt another person's feelings, do something wrong, fail to keep a promise, or lose or damage another person's belongings, etc. In these cases, writing an apology letter is one way to admit your mistake and express your regret.

The following are some guidelines for writing apology letters.

1. Express your apology or show your regret directly and sincerely.
2. Explain your actions and the reasons.
3. Propose a solution to make up for the damage or loss.
4. At the conclusion of the letter, ask for forgiveness and understanding and promise not to make the same mistake again.
5. Emphasize how much you hope the relationship will not be damaged.

Here are some other suggestions for writing apology letters.

1. An apology letter should be sent as quickly as possible after the event which you are apologizing for happens.
2. The tone, style, and wording depend not only on the seriousness of the situation but also on the relationship between the sender and the receiver.
3. The letter should be short and to the point.

The following are some commonly used expressions of apology:

- I'm terribly/very sorry.
- Pardon me.
- It was all my fault.
- How stupid/careless of me to . . .
- I owe you an apology.
- Please excuse/forgive my ignorance/rudeness.
- Please don't be mad at me.
- Please accept my sincerest apology.

 **Example**

The following is a letter of apology written by Jimmy, who offended his mother with something he said. He wrote this letter to her to show how bad he felt.

Dec. 10, 2016

Dear Mom,

I'm sorry for what I said to you last night. I shouldn't have talked back to you like that. I don't know why I lost control of my temper. Maybe it is because I've had a heavy workload these days.

I know you and Dad care about me and have done everything you could for me. I really appreciate it. I also know that you and Dad expect a lot of me. I'll study harder and try to live up to your expectations and realize my own dreams, too. Mom, please forgive me. I love you, and I am very grateful to you for all you have done for me. I promise never to make the same mistake again.

Your son,

Jimmy

Exercise A

Write down the phrases that can be used in making apologies.

1. _____

2. _____

3. _____

4. _____

參考答案請參閱解答本 p. 9

 **Exercise B**

If you fail to keep an appointment, what are some possible reasons or excuses you could offer and how will you make up for it? Write down your answers in the boxes below.

	The reason or excuse	The way to make up for it
1.		
2.		
3.		

參考答案請參閱解答本 p. 9

Exercise C

Helen borrowed a camera from her best friend, Joseph, last week to take on a trip. However, on the trip she lost the camera. Write Helen's letter of apology to Joseph.

_____
_____
_____
_____

參考答案請參閱解答本 p. 9

V. Thank-you Letters

There is a variety of situations in which you should express thanks. For example, gifts, invitations, assistance, information, and suggestions you have received are all reasons for thanks. To express thanks, a thank-you letter is more polite than just saying "thank you." Thank-you letters should be sent promptly after the event you benefit from.

The following are some tips for writing thank-you letters.

1. Express your thanks at the beginning of the letter.

2. A thank-you letter does not need to be long. Make it to the point.

3. Briefly and vividly describe what you want to thank the receiver of the letter for.

4. Explain what you have learned or how you have benefited.

5. If you have received a gift, explain how much you like it and how helpful it will be.

6. Express thanks again and include your best wishes at the conclusion of the letter.

7. The style, tone, and wording of thank-you letters may be formal or informal depending on whom you wish to show thanks to.

Here are some commonly used expressions for showing thanks:

· Thank you for your kindness/help/hospitality/etc.
· I would like to express my thanks/appreciation/ gratitude to . . . (for . . .)
· It was very kind/thoughtful of you to give me . . .
· How nice/thoughtful you were to . . .
· How nice/thoughtful of you to . . .
· I (greatly) appreciate your . . .
· It was a pleasure/an honor for me to . . .

Example

The following is a thank-you letter written by Ariel. She wrote this letter to the librarian, Mr. Ruth, to show her gratitude for his help.

Sept. 30, 2016

Dear Mr. Ruth,

　　Thank you for taking the time and trouble to help me find the books and information I needed for my report. Without your help, I wouldn't have been able to hand it in on time.

　　I used to go to the library to borrow novels. This was the first time I had gone to the library for a class. I never thought that I would have a hard time finding what I wanted.

　　You taught me how to make good use of the library. I realize that I can go to the library for many more things than just fun reading. By taking advantage of the library with your help, I have learned more than I expected. Thanks for your patience and your great help. What's more, I'm glad that I have made a new friend.

　　　　　　　　Best wishes,
　　　　　　　　Ariel

Exercise A

Think of a sentence to appropriately respond to each of the following situations. The first one has been done for you.

○ ○ ○ ○ ○ ○ ○ ○ ○ ○ ○ ○ ○ ○ ○ ○ ○ ○ ○ ○

1. You were invited to stay at your friend's house for a few days.
   Thank you so much for your hospitality/kindness.

2. Your best friend held a birthday party for you.

3. Your teacher gave you some very helpful advice.

4. Your neighbor gave you an unexpected Christmas gift.

_____

參考答案請參閱解答本 p. 9

Exercise B

You got what you had longed for on your birthday. Write a thank-you letter to the person who gave you the gift.

參考答案請參閱解答本 p. 9～10

Unit 19

Comparison and Contrast

A comparison-contrast paragraph is about the similarities and differences between two or more people, places, things, or ideas. The paragraph usually begins with a topic sentence. Comparisons show similarities between two or more people, places, or things, while contrasts show differences between them. We make comparisons and contrast whenever we consider similarities and differences.

📖 Examples ▷

- Keeping a pet is **like** raising a child.
- Rabbits, **unlike** most other animals, touch the ground with their back feet first when they are running.

Brainstorm

Before writing a comparison-contrast paragraph, you can brainstorm by creating a Venn diagram (文氏圖), and then develop a chart to list the features of each subject you are exploring.

📖 Examples ▷

- Venn Diagram

Subject A: Pet Dogs   **Subject B: Pet Cats**

1. cost more
2. more dependent on their owners and require more time of their owners
3. require more attention of their owners

1. both can serve as pets
2. both cost money
3. both need their owners' time
4. both require attention of their owners

1. cost less
2. more independent from their owners and require less time of their owners
3. require less attention of their owners

· Chart

	Subject A: Pet Dogs	**Subject B: Pet Cats**
feature 1: cost	more food	less food
feature 2: time	require being walked and washed	do not need to be washed or go outside
feature 3: attention	enjoy being part of their owners' lives	enjoy some alone time

Exercise A

Show the similarities and differences between living in a city and living in the country in the form of a Venn diagram and in the form of a chart.

· Venn Diagram

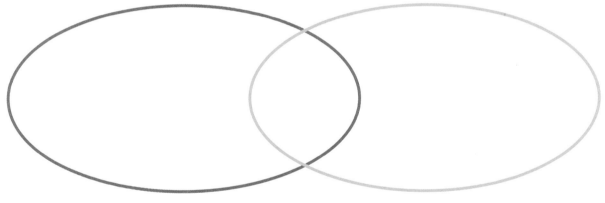

Subject A: Living in a City   Subject B: Living in the Country

· Chart

	Subject A: Living in a City	**Subject B: Living in the Country**
feature 1: _____		
feature 2: _____		
feature 3: _____		

參考答案請參閱解答本 p. 10

Transitional words or phrases that are often used in a comparison-contrast paragraph can be categorized as follows:

1. Indicating similarities:

> like, similar to, the same as, both, just as, as well as, likewise, similarly, in the same way, have something in common, also, too, etc.

2. Indicating a contrast:

> unlike, although, despite, in spite of, on the contrary, however, otherwise, nevertheless, different from, but, yet, while, on the other hand, compared to, etc.

Exercise B

Complete the following sentences by using proper transitional words or phrases. The first one has been done for you.

1. Henry is _____*like*_____ his brother in appearance. It's hard to tell the difference in their looks.

2. The food in the restaurant is delicious. _____, the atmosphere is excellent.

3. _____ the two cameras look similar, one is much more expensive than the other.

4. Bright colors make people feel happy, _____ dark ones make them feel gloomy.

5. I agree with George. My opinion is exactly _____ his.

6. The language spoken in private is usually _____ that used in public. The latter is more formal.

參考答案請參閱解答本 p. 10

A comparison-contrast paragraph is often used to persuade readers and to support a certain point of view. Keep in mind that the two (or more) items compared or contrasted should be of the same general type. That is, you can compare and contrast Japanese food and Korean food, but you can't compare and contrast a car and a pair of shoes.

Below are the steps toward writing an effective comparison-contrast paragraph.

1. Brainstorming: Gather the information you need, and group individual items together according to shared features. For example, if you want to compare and contrast positive thinkers and negative thinkers, you can come up with a chart like this:

	Subject A: Positive Thinkers	Subject B: Negative Thinkers
feature 1: feeling	happy	unhappy
feature 2: state of mind	optimistic	pessimistic
feature 3: expectations	the best	the worst

2. After selecting and organizing your items of information, you can begin to write your comparison-contrast paragraph by following either of these methods:

(1) **The Block Method/The Subject-by-subject Method**

When you apply the block method, you write down all the features of Subject A in one paragraph. Then, write another paragraph that includes all the features of Subject B, introduced in the same order of the corresponding items in the first paragraph.

(2) **The Point-by-point Method**

In this method, you compare and contrast Subject A and B according to the first feature and then the second, continuing this way paragraph by paragraph until it is completed.

The Block Method	The Point-by-point Method

Subject A: Positive Thinkers
  feature 1: feeling
  feature 2: state of mind
  feature 3: expectations
Subject B: Negative Thinkers
  feature 1: feeling
  feature 2: state of mind
  feature 3: expectations
	feature 1: feeling
	  Subject A: happy
	  Subject B: unhappy
	feature 2: state of mind
	  Subject A: optimistic
	  Subject B: pessimistic
	feature 3: expectations
	  Subject A: the best
	  Subject B: the worst

3. After gathering and organizing your information, you can start writing a comparison-contrast paragraph with any of the following topic sentence structures.

- There are similarities and differences between A and B.
- A and B have some things in common, but they behave differently.
- Even though A is similar to B, they are not identical.
- Although A and B have similar styles, they are different.
- A and B differ in three ways.

4. Use proper transitional words or phrases to connect details.

Exercise C

Read the following paragraph, find the contrasts in it, and complete the chart and the question below.

Living in a city and living in the country differ in the following three ways. First, living in a city, one can enjoy all the conveniences, such as mass transportation and shopping malls, while traveling around or doing the shopping is relatively difficult for those who live in the country. As for the environment, unlike the quiet and peaceful countryside, the hustle and bustle of a city often makes its residents feel stressed, which can affect their health. In addition, the pace of life in a city is much faster than that in the country. However, when it comes to job opportunities, the country can't compare with a city because there are many stores, companies, and government institutions in a city where jobs can be found more easily. No wonder so many young people in the country leave their homes and move to a city to seek jobs. All in all, there are advantages and disadvantages of living in a city or in the country, and the choice of where to live depends on one's personal needs.

I.

The topic sentence		
The supporting ideas	feature 1	
	feature 2	
	feature 3	
	feature 4	
The concluding sentence		
Transitional words or phrases		

II. Which method does the author use to present the details in this comparison-contrast paragraph?

參考答案請參閱解答本 p. 10

**Exercise D**

Write a comparison-contrast paragraph that starts with the topic sentence "College graduates and high school graduates differ in the following ways." Include the given information and use proper transitional words or phrases to show the relationship between sentences and details.

1. Brainstorm

	college graduates	high school graduates
feature 1: age	about 22	around 18
feature 2: attitudes to graduation	1. College graduates are under greater pressure because they need to decide whether to find a job or pursue further study. 2. There are much fewer job opportunities than before, which adds to the burdens college graduates face.	1. High school graduates are more enthusiastic because it symbolizes their growing independence. 2. Most parents allow high school students to study in other towns or even in other countries because they are no longer considered children.

2. The Topic Sentence

College graduates and high school graduates differ in the following ways.

3. Write a Paragraph

College graduates and high school graduates differ in the following ways.

_____

_____

_____

_____

_____

_____

_____

_____

參考答案請參閱解答本 p. 11

Cause and Effect

A paragraph that analyzes the causes or effects of a situation explains why something has happened (the causes) or what has happened as a result (the effects). A cause-and-effect paragraph explains the reasons for or causes of something, or it describes its results or effects.

📖 Examples

- Kevin didn't know the cake on the table was left to his sister. **Therefore**, he ate it all.
- Bob was wearing his earphones with loud music on while walking on the street. **As a result**, he didn't notice that a car sounded its horn at him.
- Jane didn't catch up the school bus **because** she got up late.

Brainstorm

Before writing a cause-and-effect paragraph, you can brainstorm and organize your ideas with either a cause-and-effect flow chart or a chart listing the causes or effects of the topic discussed.

📖 Examples

- Cause-and-effect Flow Chart (cause → effects)

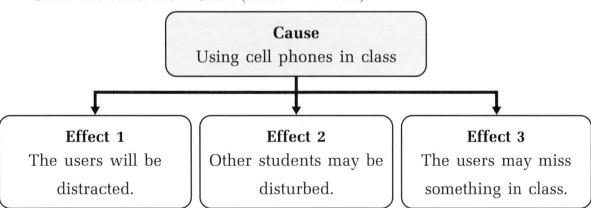

• Chart (effects ← cause)

Effect	Causes
The decision to have an abortion	1. The fetal ultrasound (超音波) shows that the baby has a fatal defect. 2. The mother herself suffers from a serious disease. 3. A woman gets pregnant because of rape.

 **Exercise A**

Write down the possible causes or effects by using both a cause-and-effect flow chart and a chart.

• Cause-and-effect Flow Chart (cause → effects)

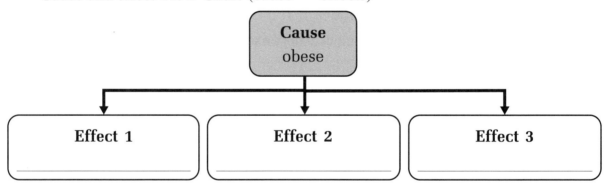

• Chart (effects ← cause)

Effect	Causes
Becoming overweight	1. _____ 2. _____ 3. _____

參考答案請參閱解答本 p. 11

Transitional words or phrases that are often used in a cause-and-effect paragraph can be categorized as follows:

1. Indicating a cause:

> as, because, since, for, because of, due to, on account of, owing to, thanks to, for this reason, etc.

2. Indicating an effect:

> so, therefore, thus, hence, as a result, as a consequence, in consequence, consequently, etc.

Exercise B

Complete the following sentences by using proper transitional words or phrases. The first one has been done for you.

1. Sandy was late for school ____*because*____ she got up late.
2. Kevin had a stomachache _____ pressure at work.
3. It rained heavily; _____, the football game was canceled.
4. Ben was sick in bed, _____ he didn't show up yesterday.
5. There has been a power failure. _____, the amusement park is not open today.

參考答案請參閱解答本 p. 11

When you write a cause-and-effect paragraph, be sure that you provide details to support the cause(s) and effect(s) you are using.

Below are the steps toward writing an effective cause-and-effect paragraph.

1. Brainstorming: Write down as many causes or effects as possible. Then, cross out the ones that are not relevant.

2. After deciding which causes or effects to use, you can start with any of the following topic sentence structures.
   - There are ... causes of/reasons for/effects of ...
   - There are ... main reasons why ...
   - ... has great/harmful/destructive effects on ...
   - One main cause/effect of ... is ...

3. Use proper transitional words or phrases to organize your ideas.

 **Example** →

Topic: The causes of global warming

1. Brainstorm

Effect	Causes
The increase of CO_2 in the atmosphere	1. Many cars, airplanes, and factories discharge huge amounts of carbon dioxide. 2. The power we use causes an increase in carbon dioxide. 3. Carbon dioxide doesn't allow the sun's heat to escape into space.

2. The Topic Sentence

There are several causes that lead to the increase of carbon dioxide in the atmosphere, the primary reason for global warming.

3. Write a Paragraph

There are several causes that lead to the increase of carbon dioxide in the atmosphere, the primary reason for global warming. First of all, many cars, airplanes, and factories burn fuels, such as oil, gas, and coal, and this results in the discharge of huge amounts of carbon dioxide into the atmosphere. What's worse, the power that people use in their homes and offices has caused an increase in the amount of carbon dioxide as well. For instance, air conditioners, refrigerators, and lights are mainly powered by carbon fuels. Carbon dioxide in the air reflects the sun's heat back to the earth and doesn't allow it to escape into space, thus causing our planet to heat up. If we do not take action soon, eventually our planet will no longer be a habitable place.

Exercise C

Fill in the following blanks with the possible effects of global warming first, and then write a cause-and-effect paragraph. Your paragraph should be more than 120 words in length.

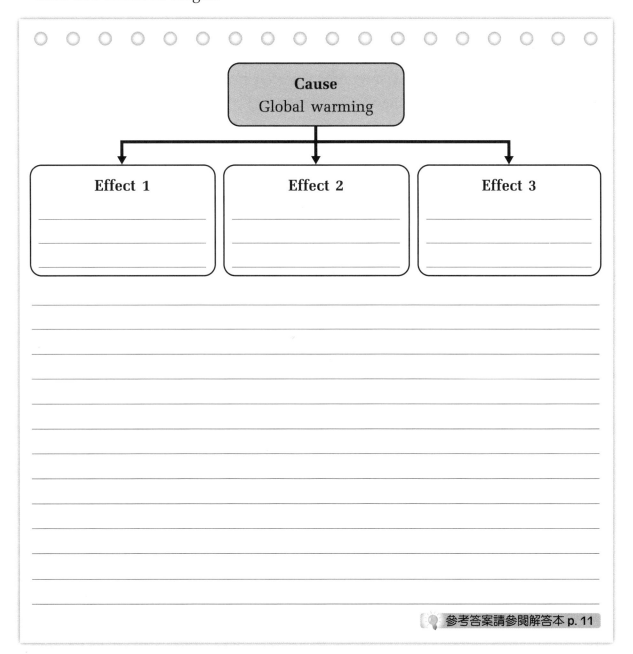

Cause
Global warming

Effect 1

Effect 2

Effect 3

參考答案請參閱解答本 p. 11

Unit 21

Expressing Opinions

In an opinion paragraph, you express your own personal opinion about a controversial (有爭議性的) topic. When writing an opinion paragraph, you need to clearly state your opinion at the very beginning and then follow it with the reasons that you support it.

Brainstorm

Before writing an opinion paragraph, you can brainstorm ideas by drawing up an OREO chart to organize your writing.

 **Example**

Topic: Should people have cosmetic surgery to improve their appearance?

O	**Opinion** • I am totally against the idea of sacrificing health in order to look good.
R	**Reason** • What's the use of being physically attractive if we are not healthy or have to risk our lives to enjoy it?
E	**Example** • Some people go so far as to have stomach surgery to restrict their food consumption, regardless of the possibility of malnutrition or fatal side effects.
O	**Opinion** • Even though looking good might strengthen one's confidence and make one feel better, it is still unwise to go to such extremes.

Exercise A

Fill out the OREO chart to complete the outline for an opinion paragraph on the given topic.

Topic: Should students wear school uniform?

O	**Opinion**

R	**Reason**
	_____
	_____
E	**Example**
	_____
	_____
O	**Opinion**
	_____
	_____

參考答案請參閱解答本 p. 11

Transitional words or phrases that are often used in an opinion paragraph can be categorized as follows:

1. Introducing personal opinions:

> as far as I am concerned, as for me, I believe/consider, in my opinion/view, from my point of view, it is my belief, it seems to me that, let me say personally, that/this is my viewpoint, etc.

2. Connecting reasons:

> The first/second reason is … , another reason is … , Firstly/Secondly … , besides, moreover, furthermore, in addition, additionally, what's more, etc.

Exercise B

Circle the correct transitional phrase for each of the following sentences. The first one has been done for you.

1. The dress looks nice, but (in my opinion; besides), it is not worth the price.

2. Young children learn quickly; (as far as I am concerned; what's more), they also remember everything they have learned.

3. First of all, I got up late. (Another reason; My viewpoint) was that I didn't catch the bus. That's why I was late for the meeting.

4. When I was little, (*in my point of view*; *it was my belief that*) there were angels in the world.

5. Many people bet that Germany will win the World Cup. (*As for me*; *In addition*), the odds are in favor of Argentina.

參考答案請參閱解答本 p. 11

You need to have an opinion about the topic before you write an opinion paragraph about it. The topic sentence should state this opinion clearly and the supporting ideas should be the reasons for your opinion. At the end, you should conclude the paragraph with a restatement of your opinion.

After coming up with examples and information to support your argument, you can start writing an opinion paragraph with one of the following sample topic sentences.

· I agree/disagree that-clause

· I agree/disagree with someone for ... reasons

· I am for/against the idea that-clause

Example

Topic: Should the book *Anne Frank's Diary* be taught to young children in schools?

1. Brainstorm

O	**Opinion** · I agree that *Anne Frank's Diary* is a good source of teaching materials.
R	**Reason** · Students can learn more about the Holocaust by reading it.
E	**Example** · By reading the words of Anne Frank and the descriptions of the people around her, students can learn about the Holocaust through an individual's voice rather than through news reports, statistics, and historical records.
R	**Reason** · There are no depictions of frightening scenes of blood and violence in the book.

E	**Example** • The diary ends when Anne was taken away from the Secret Annex, with no further description of her sufferings or the suffering of other Jews in the concentration camps.
R	**Reason** • The book conveys a message of hope and compassion.
E	**Example** • Even when Anne was confined to the hiding place, she still maintained a positive attitude and expressed great sympathy for those who suffered.
O	**Opinion** • To sum up, *Anne Frank's Diary* is an excellent choice of reading materials for teaching the Holocaust.

2. Write a Paragraph

Though some teachers oppose the idea of using *Anne Frank's Diary* in the classrooms, I feel that it is a good text for teaching. First of all, through it, students can better understand the Holocaust. By reading about the situation of Anne Frank and the people in her diary, students learn about the Holocaust through an individual's voice rather than through news reports, statistics, and historical records. Besides, young readers will feel closer to Anne and relate with her. At the same time, students will not be confronted with the violence and horror of the Holocaust. The diary ends with Anne and her family being taken away from the Secret Annex but with no further description of the sufferings of the Jews in the concentration camps. Even without such terrifying details, students are still able to understand the horrifying reality that Anne experienced. Most importantly, the book conveys a message of hope and compassion. Even when Anne was confined to the hiding place, she still maintained a positive attitude and expressed great sympathy for those who were suffering. To sum up, *Anne Frank's Diary* is an excellent choice for teaching young people about the Holocaust.

Exercise C

Write an opinion paragraph on the given topic. Brainstorm ideas by filling out the OREO chart first, and then develop your ideas into a paragraph.

Topic: Does Facebook bring people together or cause them to be even further apart?

1. Brainstorm

O	**Opinion** _____ _____
R	**Reason** _____ _____
E	**Example** _____ _____
O	**Opinion** _____ _____

2. Write a Paragraph

_____
_____
_____
_____
_____
_____
_____
_____
_____
_____

參考答案請參閱解答本 p. 11～12

Writing About a Graph or a Chart

Sometimes, it is a good idea to include a relevant graph or chart in your writing to present information in a readily understandable way. Types of charts include bar graphs, pie charts, diagrams, tables, and flow charts. Writing about a graph or chart requires writers to select and report the main features of the data, explain their significance, and to point out trends in the information. You can also make comparisons based on the data or describe a process. Paragraphs about charts should begin with a topic sentence that provides an overview of the rest of the paragraph.

Example

The table below shows the main reasons why people do their shopping at Ian's Supermarket. The total 160 interviewees include 81men and 79 women.

Reasons for shopping at Ian's Supermarket	No. of men	No. of women
close to home (location)	25	20
competitive prices	14	17
good reputation	17	22
sufficient parking spaces	21	20
24-hour shopping	4	0

The table above shows the main reasons why people do their shopping at Ian's Supermarket. Of these five reasons, location, reputation, and availability of parking are the top ones. Men consider location to be the most important factor because they prefer to save time by shopping closer to home. On the other hand, women shop at Ian's Supermarket because of its good reputation, for a good reputation generally means that quality and service are also good.

**Exercise**

The pie chart below shows how an average British home uses electricity. Write a two-paragraph essay on this topic. In the first paragraph, summarize the information presented in the chart, and then write about how electricity is consumed in your own home in the second paragraph.

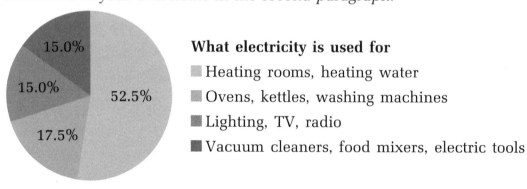

What electricity is used for

- Heating rooms, heating water
- Ovens, kettles, washing machines
- Lighting, TV, radio
- Vacuum cleaners, food mixers, electric tools

參考答案請參閱解答本 p. 12

Definition

A definition explains the meaning of a word or term. Some terms are concrete (具體的) and have definite meanings; others are abstract (抽象的) and the definition may differ from person to person, such as "happiness," "love," "hope," etc. Using definition is one of the strategies to develop the content. Definition can be made in terms of "what," "when," "where," "how," and "why."

The following are some approaches to define a term.

- Explain what it is or how it looks.
- Explain the characteristics, personality, or components.
- Explain the origin, reason, or the purpose.
- Link it to something familiar to make the term easier to understand.
- Contrast it with something else, so differences between the two help clarify the meaning.
- Use facts, information, examples, personal experience, or stories to support the definition.

Example A

An area code is a section of a telephone number which generally represents the geographical area that the phone receiving the call is based in. It is the two or three digits just before the local number. If the number being called is in the same area as the number making the call, an area code usually doesn't need to be dialed. The local number, on the other hand, must always be dialed entirely.

The definition in this paragraph includes:

1. What is an area code?

   (1) An area code is a section of a telephone number.

   (2) An area code represents the geographical area that the phone receiving the call is based in.

2. How an area code is formed?

There are two or three digits just before the local number.

3. When an area code should be used?

An area code should be dialed if the number being called is not in the same area as the number making the call.

📖 Example B ▶

There are two kinds of heroes: heroes who shine in the face of great danger, who perform an amazing act in a difficult situation, and heroes who live an ordinary life like us, who do their work unnoticed by many of us, but who make a difference in the lives of others.

Heroes are selfless people who perform extraordinary acts. The mark of heroes is not necessarily the result of their action, but what they are willing to do for others and for their chosen cause. Even if they fail, their determination lives on for others to follow. The glory lies not in the achievement but in the sacrifice.

From the above definition essay, we learn that definition essay may include the following:

1. What are the two kinds of heroes?

the 1st paragraph (→ *the definition of the term*)

2. How are heroes different from ordinary people? What do they do?

the 2nd paragraph (→ *the characteristic and personality*)

3. What is the mark of heroes?

the 2nd and 3rd sentences of the 2nd paragraph (→ *the importance or influence on others or on the society*)

4. What does their glory lie in?

the last sentence of the essay (→ *Why is it (are they) honored and remembered?*)

Exercise A

Define the following terms in three different ways.

1. growing up

   (A) _____

   (B) _____

   (C) _____

2. a true friend

   (A) _____

   (B) _____

   (C) _____

參考答案請參閱解答本 p. 12

Transitional words or phrases that are often used in a definition paragraph can be categorized as follows:

1. **Showing similarity:**

   like, in the same way, similarly, as, just as, in other words, that is, that is to say, to put it another way, etc.

2. **Showing difference:**

   unlike, on the contrary, by/in comparison, by/in contrast, however, nevertheless, etc.

3. **Indicating addition:**

   besides, in addition (to), moreover, furthermore, what's more/better/worse, etc.

4. **Giving examples:**

   such as, for example/instance, take ... as an example, etc.

Exercise B

Complete the following sentences by using proper transitional words or phrases.

1. Some people say "necessity is the mother of invention." _____, if something is needed, then it will be invented.

2. Making friends can be a lot like making soup. To develop a close friendship requires many different ingredients. _____, trust and similar interests are very important. _____, constant care is also needed.

3. A saying goes, "Out of sight, out of mind." _____, if we don't see someone, we don't think of him or her so often. _____, this is not always the case. _____, a true friend is forever. No matter how far away he or she is, he or she is always in our mind.

參考答案請參閱解答本 p. 12

Example

Write a definition essay on "Growing Up." Brainstorm first, and then write a rough outline. Develop the ideas, organize them, and bring the essay to an end with a conclusion.

1. Brainstorm

(1. When is it? 2. What's the difference? 3. meaning? 4. your experience and attitude 5. How do you feel?)

2. Write a Rough Outline

1st paragraph:

The topic sentence: Generally speaking, when a person turns seventeen, he or she is considered "not a child."

2nd paragraph:

The topic sentence: How was I aware that I was no longer a "kid"?

The supporting ideas: (1. being independent 2. making one's own decisions 3. being sensible and reasonable 4. being treated as a grownup)

Concluding paragraph:

The topic sentence: Little by little, I come to realize that "a grownup" means being independent, responsible, sensible and reasonable.

The supporting ideas: being wise and showing concern not only for themselves

3. Write an Essay

Growing Up

Generally speaking, when a person turns seventeen, he or she is considered "not a child." In other words, that person has reached maturity and become a "grown-up." He or she can no longer enjoy the benefit of being a child such as doing something silly, doing something wrong without being punished or having his or her own way.

How was I aware that I was no more a "kid"? On the first day of going to senior high school, I was waiting for my father to take me to the school. He said to me, "It's time. Go now or you'll be late. Don't ride your bike too fast." "Won't you drive me to school?" "Well, you have grown up. You have to be independent and do what you have to do." When I asked my parents what club I had to join, they answered, "That's your business. You have to make your own decision." When I complained, they told me to be sensible. When I got angry, they told me to be reasonable. They no longer make plans for me. Instead, they begin to ask my opinions and think much of my judgment.

Little by little, I come to realize that "a grownup" means being independent, responsible, sensible and reasonable. Grownups must be wise enough to balance between work and play, emotion and ration. Grownups must show concern not only for themselves and their family members but for others and the society as well. I'm glad that I am on my way from being a "green" to a "ripe" grownup.

 **Exercise C**

It's your turn to write a definition essay on "Happiness." Take the example essay "Growing Up" as an example. Before writing the essay, brainstorm first, and then prepare a rough outline. Develop your ideas, organize them, and bring the essay to an end with a conclusion.

○ ○ ○ ○ ○ ○ ○ ○ ○ ○ ○ ○ ○ ○ ○ ○ ○ ○ ○ ○

_____

參考答案請參閱解答本 p. 12～13

Unit 24

Giving Reasons

In Unit 20, we learn about Cause and Effect. A cause and effect essay describes "A leads to B." It describes something (A) happens and what (B) happens as a result. Such essays tell the readers the link between A (cause) and B (result) or how or why things happen. In this unit, we will learn "Giving Reasons." A reason-giving essay mainly explains to the readers why, the reason(s) for something. It can be used to explain an event, a phenomenon or to make comments. It's one of the most common skills for writing because there's always a reason for something to have happened, or for something to be done or not to be done. Besides, when you have to convince others of a certain fact, a point of view, the truth or advisability of something, you should also give reasons.

The following are some ways to give reasons.

- By presenting the views of experts.
- By using data, statistics, or research.
- By referring to a report, an event or a situation that actually occurred.
- By making an analysis or judgment.
- By offering personal views, experience or appealing to emotions.
- By making use of knowledge and common sense.

Examples

Give reasons for each of the following statements.

1. Effects of colors can be applied to many parts of our daily life.

   a. School buses and taxis are painted yellow.

   → Yellow is bright enough to attract people's attention.

   b. Stop signs are painted red.

   → Red is a color usually used to indicate warning.

   c. Most fast-food restaurants are decorated in bright colors.

   → According to studies, bright colors can increase people's appetites because bright colors are the natural colors of many foods.

   → Bright colors are able to raise people's spirits.

2. A sense of inferiority has a negative influence on a person.

→ People who are bound to be confronted with an identity crisis may cheapen themselves in the course of time.

→ A sense of inferiority can turn into mental scars, which may also bruise their egos, shake their confidence, and hence, affect how they value themselves.

→ People without confidence are unlikely to do anything well. They may be blamed or neglected. As a result, they will become even less confident.

 Exercise A

Think of at least three reasons to support each of the following statements. The first one has been done for you.

1. Children should not watch too much TV.
   (A) *Children don't know how to choose programs.*
   (B) *Many TV programs involve sex or violence.*
   (C) *Watching too much TV may do harm to their eyes and health.*

2. We should try to get rid of the habit of putting things off.
   (A) _____
   _____
   (B) _____
   _____
   (C) _____
   _____

3. Failure is the mother of success.
   (A) _____
   _____
   (B) _____
   _____
   (C) _____
   _____

參考答案請參閱解答本 p. 13

Transitional words or phrases that are often used in a reason-giving paragraph can be categorized as follows:

1. Showing reasons:

because, since, because of, due to, thanks to, owing to, for one thing, etc.

2. Giving more reasons:

also, besides, in addition, moreover, furthermore, second(ly), also, what's more, what's better/worse, most important of all, best/worst of all, etc.

3. Showing results:

in this way, otherwise, as a result, therefore, in consequence, hence, etc.

Exercise B

Complete the following sentences by using proper transitional words or phrases.

1. Sunburn is caused by invisible rays from the sun. These harmful rays may cause pain and swelling. _____ , they may cause first-degree or second-degree burns. _____ , severe sunburn may result in permanent damage to the skin.

2. There are many reasons why I love English class the most. _____ , our teacher is so humorous that she makes me feel learning English is interesting. _____ , she doesn't blame us for not being able to answer the questions. Instead, she gives us a number of hints in an interesting way. _____ , we can always figure out the answer without feeling embarrassed.

3. Convenience stores in Taiwan are popular _____ the vast variety of services that they provide. _____ buying necessities, people can also pay their phone bills, parking fees, traffic fines, and so on. _____ , they can withdraw or deposit money at the ATMs installed in these stores. _____ , people are able to preorder

many different items, ranging from local cuisine to concert tickets, in convenience stores. _____, these services are available around the clock _____ convenience stores are open twenty-four hours.

參考答案請參閱解答本 p.13

The following are the steps toward writing an effective reason-giving essay.

1. Clearly point out the topic in the introductory paragraph.

2. Give supporting ideas.

3. Develop each supporting idea by giving details or examples.

4. Present the reasons in logical order, such as the order of time, steps, space, importance, or difficulty.

5. Conclude by summarizing the main points or emphasizing the reasons.

 Example

Topic: Taiwan has the highest density of convenience stores in the world.

Facts:

→ Sometimes, two branches of the same convenience store can be found on the same block.

→ Even in Taiwan's quiet suburbs, there is always at least one convenience store open for business.

1. Brainstorm

First, list all the possible reasons which come to your mind. Then, cross out what is unnecessary or unimportant and organize the reasons to support the topic. Lastly, make a conclusion based on the reasons.

2. Organization of the essay

reasons	details
a variety of services	① daily necessities, snacks, drinks, etc. ② pay bills, parking fees, traffic fines, tax, etc. ③ withdraw or deposit money at the ATMs installed in these stores ④ "pay-on-pickup" service ⑤ book railway tickets

marketing strategies	a variety of services, commercials, promotions, discounts, new products, etc.
others	not far away, polite clerks, opening 24 hours, etc.

3. Write an Essay

Taiwan has the highest density of convenience stores in the world. Sometimes, two branches of the same convenience store can be found on the same block. Even in Taiwan's quiet suburbs, there is always at least one convenience store open for business.

Convenience stores in Taiwan offer a variety of services. We can buy almost all the necessities there such as daily necessities, snacks and drinks. Besides, we can pay our phone bills, parking fees, traffic fines, taxes and so on. We can also withdraw or deposit money at the ATMs installed in the convenience stores. Best of all, convenience stores offer "pay-on-pickup" service, thus saving us a lot of time. Booking railway tickets is another important service convenience stores offer.

Convenience stores combine regular service with special sales promotions once in a while. In this way, many people are tempted to frequent and spend money at the convenience stores.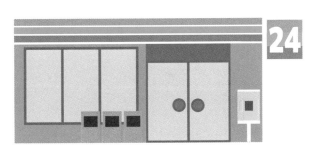

Exercise C

Follow the given topics below and write an essay for each topic including the introduction, the supporting ideas, and the conclusion.

1. Topic: Saying "No" to Drugs

_____

_____

_____

2. Topic: The Person Who Influences me the Most

參考答案請參閱解答本 p. 13

Unit 25

Providing Examples

Providing examples is a very common writing strategy. Examples are provided to clarify a difficult idea, to provide supporting ideas, to back up the main idea, and most important of all, to make the idea clearer and more comprehensible for the reader. Some sources of examples are as follows:

· Personal experience or observation
· Examples taken from famous, great or well-known people
· Wise sayings or quotations
· Facts or reports from books, studies, newspapers, and magazines

Examples

Give two or three examples to each of the following topics.

· The same gesture carries different meanings in different countries.
  → Forming a circle with the thumb and the index finger means "OK" in the U.S.A.; however, it is an offensive gesture in Brazil.
  → Nodding one's head is a negative answer in Bulgaria, while most people in other parts of the world shake their heads to show disagreement.

· The first time I made a speech in public, I was very nervous.
  → As I stood there looking at the audience, my heart was actually in my mouth.
  → I felt a thundering herd of elephants in my stomach.
  → Nervousness filled my veins, making me light-headed.

· Senior High school life is busy.
  → Students have a lot of tests to take and a lot of homework to do.
  → Students are required to take part in at least one club or extracurricular activity.
  → On holidays, students may be asked to do something for their community or take part in community activities.

Exercise A

Think of two or three examples to support each of the following topics. The first one has been done for you.

1. Never giving up is the key to success.

   (A) *Never giving up means keeping on working. That is, "strong will." Where there is a will, "there is a way."*

   (B) *Before Edison successfully invented electric light bulbs, he had failed hundreds of times.*

   (C) *As a wise saying goes, "Constant dropping wears away the stone."*

2. Obesity can pose a serious threat to one's health.

   (A) _____

   _____

   (B) _____

   _____

   (C) _____

   _____

3. My mom is the kindest person in the world.

   (A) _____

   _____

   (B) _____

   _____

   (C) _____

   _____

4. Jason is very selfish.

   (A) _____

   (B) _____

   (C) _____

參考答案請參閱解答本 p. 14

Transitional words or phrases used to weave the supporting details together can be categorized as follows:

1. **Listing examples:**

> for example, for instance, such as, including, especially, specifically, particularly, etc.

2. **Listing the first example:**

> to begin with, for one thing, first, firstly, etc.

3. **Introducing more examples:**

> take ... as another example, more importantly, most importantly, most important of all, besides, also, moreover, in addition, furthermore, what's more/worse/better, worse still, last, finally, etc.

4. **Showing contrast or different examples:**

> however, while, unlike, but, on the contrary, etc.

Exercise B

Complete the following sentences by using proper transitional words or phrases.

1. Cultures differ from country to country. _____, most Americans show affection by kissing and hugging _____ most Asians are not used to such close contact. Most of them greet each other by smiling, nodding their head or shaking hands.

2. As far as I am concerned, senior high school is more fun than junior high. _____, most teachers consider us "young adults." _____, we can always make decisions on our own and should be responsible for ourselves. _____, we often make fun of each other and share cookies and drinks with each other. _____, we have fun playing balls almost every day after school.

3. Going to Bali was the most relaxing vacation that I have ever had. _____, I slept away half the morning without the disturbance of my alarm clock—I could finally stop being an early bird. _____, all I did was chill out. With some interesting stories and soothing music, I lay on the chaise longue (躺椅), enjoying the gentle breeze. _____, I turned off my cell phone so that I wouldn't get any calls from work.

參考答案請參閱解答本 p. 14

Examples provided to back up the main idea and topic sentence should be concrete, clear, and relevant to the topic. One or several examples can be provided for the topic.

The following are the ways to present examples:

1. **In time order:** starting from the earliest example

   Example

   • The world is changing very fast. In 1998 Kodak had 170,000 employees and sold 85% of all photo paper worldwide. However, with the emergence of digital camera, their business model disappeared rapidly and they got bankrupt. And now, we have the cell phone with built-in camera, which makes it easy for us to take pictures anytime, anywhere.

2. **In spatial order:** from left to right or right to left; from top to bottom or bottom to top; from distant to near or near to distant

   Example

   • This special building is sure to catch your eye. The outside of the tall building has black and white stripes painted, which you can see in the distance. In front of the door is a statue of a general riding a horse. On entering, you will find a large garden with different species of flowers growing throughout the year.

3. **In order of importance:** from the most important point to the least one or from the least important to the most important one

   Example

   • Artificial Intelligence is sure to influence a lot of industries. In the US, young lawyers already don't get jobs. Because of IBM Watson, you can get legal advice within seconds with 90% accuracy compared with 70% accuracy when done by humans. Watson already helps nurses diagnose cancer four times more accurate than human nurses. Facebook has a pattern recognition software that can recognize faces better than humans. In 2030, computers will become more intelligent than humans.

Organization of an example-providing essay

Introductory paragraph	Introduce the topic and main idea of the essay.
Supporting ideas	Provide one or more examples to support the topic.
Conclusion	Make a summary or briefly repeat the supporting ideas and then make the conclusion or express the result.

 **Example**

Topic: Stereotypes

The Topic Sentence: Thinking in stereotypes can lead to unfair judgments.

The Supporting Ideas:

① When we think in stereotypes, we neglect the differences among individuals. Our minds automatically produce a stereotyped picture instead of a real one.

Example I: the stereotype of taxi drivers: middle-aged, talkative, male

Example II: the stereotype of adolescents: showing no respect for their elders, having poor manners, sloppy speech, not realizing how much they have

② Facts become distorted and wrong decisions are made.

The Concluding Sentence: Stereotypes are too simple to be fair to people, so we should not rely on them too much.

Exercise C

Now, it's your turn to write an example-providing essay. First outline your paragraphs, then think of examples to support the topic. Develop and organize the examples into an essay. Finally, bring the essay to an end with a convincing conclusion.

Topic: Saying "No"

1. Write a Rough Outline

The Topic Sentence: _____

The Supporting Ideas:

_____

_____

The Conclusion: _____

2. Write an Essay

_____

_____

_____

_____

_____

_____

_____

_____

_____

_____

_____

_____

_____

參考答案請參閱解答本 p. 14

Unit 26

Process

The main purpose of a process paragraph is to explain how a task is performed or how to deal with a problem step by step. Process writing is important in describing a recipe, scientific writing, task to be done, or a problem to be solved. A good process paragraph should include clear instructions or steps so that the readers can easily follow the steps required to carry out the task successfully.

The following are the steps toward writing an effective process paragraph.

1. First, write a topic sentence to state what the process aims for, give background information of the process or outline the process.

2. Use imperative structures or sentences (祈使句) to introduce the steps. Sentences used to introduce the steps are as follows:

   · Here are ways to ...
   · There are some steps you can follow.
   · The following are the steps.
   · The steps you have to take are as follows.

3. Clarify the process or each step by explaining or giving examples.

4. Present each step in order of time, place, difficulty, or importance.

Transitional words or phrases that are often used in a process paragraph can be categorized as follows:

1. Showing a series of steps:

> first, first of all, second, third, last, next, then, after that, besides, in addition (to), finally, the last step, etc.

2. Showing more steps or the connection between steps:

> before, after, not ... until, while, as, at the same time, meanwhile, for example, for instance, etc.

3. Showing emphasis or serving as a reminder:

> what is more important, most important of all, remember to . . . , be sure to . . . , never. . . , don't . . . , etc.

Organization of a Process Essay

Introductory paragraph	Topic sentence : What to be introduced
One or more paragraphs (if the process is complicated)	Clearly describe "How" step by step. Give explanation or examples.
Conclusion	Summarize the main steps of the process, briefly describe the result, make brief comments or give personal opinions.

📖 Example A ▶

Below are the steps to follow in making a salad. Write a process paragraph based on the steps.

A. Get some of your favorite vegetables, such as lettuce, broccoli, onions, or cucumber.

B. Wash the vegetables.

C. Chop the vegetables into bite-sized pieces and put them into a big bowl.

D. You can add some fruit, such as raisins or sliced apples, and some nuts, such as walnuts or almonds.

E. Add your favorite dressing and mix all the ingredients together.

How to Make a Delicious Salad

Salad is one of my family's favorite dishes. It is not at all difficult to make a delicious and healthy salad. **First**, choose the vegetables. I usually use lettuce, broccoli, onions, and cucumber. **Then**, wash the vegetables. **Next**, chop the vegetables into bite-sized pieces and **then** put them all into a big bowl. I also like to add fruit such as raisins or sliced apples along with walnuts, almonds, or other nuts. **Finally**, I add my favorite dressing and toss all the ingredients together. In less than an hour, the salad is ready.

📖 *Example B*

Write a process paragraph. The following are the steps for the first aid for burns; however, they are out of order. Put the steps in order and then use proper transitional words or phrases to link the sentences.

A. Cool the injured area in cool running water for at least twenty minutes.

B. Cover the burn loosely with a clean blanket.

C. If necessary, call an ambulance and send the injured to the hospital.

D. If any clothing is wet or affected, remove it from the injured area quickly.

E. Soak the injured area in cool water for at least twenty minutes.

First Aid for Burns

First, cool the injured area in cool running water for at least twenty minutes. Then, if any clothing is wet or affected, remove it from the injured area quickly. Next, soak the injured area in cool water for at least twenty minutes. The fourth step is to cover the burn loosely with a clean blanket. Finally, if necessary, call an ambulance and send the injured person to the hospital.

✎ Exercise A

Write a process essay on "How to Prepare for an Interview". Below are the steps to prepare for an interview. Develop these steps into a process essay.

A. Do the research and make sure you understand what the interview is all about.

B. Prepare what you may respond to the interviewer.

C. Make sure you wear properly.

D. Remember not to talk too much or too little.

E. Be confident but not too proud.

F. Making a good impression is important.

💡 參考答案請參閱解答本 p. 14～15

Exercise B

Write a process essay on "How to Plan a Party".

参考答案請參閱解答本 p. 15

 **Unit 27**

Problems and Solutions

A problem-solving essay is to describe a problem, explain its background, and come up with possible solutions. The problem may be a dilemma (左右為難), a conflict, a difficult task, an obstacle to be overcome, or just something to be done. Problems occur in every aspect of our life, ranging from personal matters, like how to improve one's English, to global concerns, such as environmental protection and the extinction of a certain species. Unlike cause-effect essays, which emphasize the link between cause and effect, problem-solution essays focus more on how to solve the problems. The solutions to the problems can be based on the following:

- theory
- logical reasoning
- case studies
- information such as statistics
- personal experience
- cases of successful solutions

 **Example**

Find out the problems in the following passage and provide the possible solutions to the problems.

- John is interested in English. He spends more time in English than in other subjects. However, his English doesn't improve much. He feels frustrated and has lost confidence in studying English.

Problem(s):

① John has difficulty in studying English.

② John feels frustrated and has lost confidence in studying English.

Possible solution(s):

① He can improve his studying method.

② He can build up his confidence.

③ He can ask his teacher for advice.

Exercise A

Write down at least two possible solutions to each of the following problems.
The first one has been done for you.

Problems	Possible solutions
generation gap	1. *Parents should try to spend more time communicating with their children.* 2. *Parents should try to keep up with the times so as to understand what young people think.* 3. *Both parents and children should try to respect each other's points of view.*
being overweight	1. _____ 2. _____ 3. _____
feeling frustrated	1. _____ 2. _____ 3. _____
Some species are in danger of extinction.	1. _____ 2. _____ 3. _____

參考答案請參閱解答本 p. 15

Transitional words or phrases that are often used in a problem-solving essay can be categorized as follows:

1. Explaining:

> for example, in fact, actually, in theory, that is (to say), in other words, on one hand, on the other hand, generally speaking, etc.

2. Showing a series of or more solutions and explanations:

> first, first of all, then, next, finally, lastly, besides, in addition, what's more, also, more/most importantly, etc.

3. Showing personal opinions or offering evidence:

> as I know, according to, a study shows/indicates . . . , based on . . . , etc.

Exercise B

I. *Fill in each blank with a transitional word.*

Brushing your teeth regularly will help you maintain a healthy smile. But that smile won't last long if you don't take proper care of your toothbrush and switch to a new one often. ¹_____ the American Dental Association (ADA), toothbrushes can harbor bacteria. These germs come from the mouth and can accumulate in toothbrushes over time.

²_____, Americans replace their toothbrushes only once or twice a year. The ADA, however, recommends using a new toothbrush every three to four months. Children's toothbrushes may need to be changed more frequently.

During those three to four months of use, there are several ways to keep a toothbrush clean. ³_____, rinse your toothbrush thoroughly with tap water after use, making sure to remove any toothpaste and debris. Store your toothbrush in an upright position, and let it air dry. ⁴_____, do not share toothbrushes.

參考答案請參閱解答本 p. 15

II. *Answer the following questions according to the above passage.*

1. What is the problem of using the same toothbrush for a long time?

_____

_____

2. How can we keep a toothbrush clean?

_____

_____

_____

參考答案請參閱解答本 p. 15

Organization of a problem-solving essay

Introductory paragraph	Present the problem, describe the background and explain who or what gets involved.
Supporting ideas (one or two paragraphs)	Define or present the problem in detail. Offer solutions and explain why and how the solution(s) will work. If there are a series of steps, present the steps in a logical order.
Conclusion	Put focus on the outcome and the influence.

📖 *Example* ▷

Write a problem-solving essay "My First Speech Contest" based on the following information.

Introductory paragraph: (→ *describe the background*)

• I was asked to attend a speech contest in the first year of senior high.

The supporting ideas: Paragraph 2 (→ *details of the problem*)

• I was frightened the first time I made a speech in public.

• I felt my heart was in my mouth.

• It seemed that the audience could hear my heart hammering.

• There were not butterflies but elephants in my stomach. They were trampling me thoroughly.

• Nervousness filled my veins, making me light-headed.

• My mind went blank.

The supporting ideas: Paragraph 3 (→ *the solution*)

• I told myself to take the audience as stones.

• I told myself that I had been well-prepared and that I had to calm down.

• I took a deep breath.

Conclusion: (→ *the result and influence*)

• The crowd began to focus their attention on my speech.

• A growing sense of confidence began to build inside me.

• My muscles relaxed and my breathing eased.

• Finally, I finished my speech and went off the stage with thunderous applause.

• I successfully finished my first speech.

My First Speech Contest

It was really an unforgettable experience. Even now, I still remember the first time I made a speech in public. It was a speech contest in the first year of senior high and I was the representative of my class.

As soon as I stood on the stage, I felt my heart was in my mouth. It seemed like the audience could hear it hammering. It was, I felt, not butterflies but elephants that were in my stomach. The thundering herd was trampling me thoroughly. Nervousness filled my veins, making me light-headed. My mind went blank.

With the audience looking at me, I told myself to take the audience as stones. Since stones couldn't hear or criticize, I calmed down a little. I told myself, "You are well-prepared. You can make it." Then, I took a deep breath and slowly I began to talk. As the crowd began to focus their attention on my speech, a growing sense of confidence began to build

inside me. My muscles relaxed and my breathing eased. Finally, I finished my speech and went off the stage with thunderous applause. Since I finished my first speech successfully, I know I have overcome my stage fright. I learn that if I am well-prepared, I will have no problem of speaking in public.

Exercise C

There are times we are misunderstood. Write a problem-solving essay explaining: (1) How or why were you misunderstood? (2) How did you solve the problem? (3) What was the result or influence on you. Your essay should be at least 120 words in length.

參考答案請參閱解答本 p. 15～16

 **Unit 28**

Making Comments

When you want to express your feelings or opinions about a book, a story, or an event, first briefly summarize what you have heard, seen, or read, and then give your response. Before you start writing, think about the following questions:

- What do I think about this story/event/issue?
- Do I like it? Why or why not?
- Which part of the story/event/issue impresses me the most?
- What point(s) in the story/event/issue do I agree or disagree with?
- What have I learned from it?

Next, following the steps below, you can put your answers into a paragraph that expresses your opinions:

1. Write a brief summary of the story/event/issue.
2. Write down your opinions from the answers you give to the questions above.
3. Use the following transitional words or phrases to organize your opinions.

> however, finally, first, in addition, from my point of view, in my opinion/view, I think that . . . , I am of the opinion that . . . , I agree/disagree that . . . , what I have learned from . . . is . . . ,etc.

 **Example**

Topic: My Reflections on "The Teacher Who Changed My Life"

1. Write a Rough Outline

The Topic Sentence: Recently, I read an article entitled "The Teacher Who Changed My Life" by Nicholas Gage.

The Supporting Ideas: ① a brief summary of the story

② the part that impresses me the most

③ what I have learned from the story

2. Write a Paragraph

Recently, I read an article entitled "The Teacher Who Changed My Life" written by Nicholas Gage. In the article, the author described in detail how his schoolteacher Marjorie Hurd inspired him to strive to become a journalist. The part that impressed me most was the way Miss Hurd spurred the author, a young war refugee, to understand the power of the written word and further, helped him put his love for his mother into words. Many of us may have met similar teachers who greatly influenced us, but very few of them are like Miss Hurd, who was able to direct the author's grief and pain into a love of learning. What I have learned from the story is that a truly good teacher is one that can help students see and realize their own potential.

Exercise

Now, it's your turn to write a paragraph to express your views about a book which impresses you the most. First, make an outline of your paragraph, then develop your ideas into complete sentences, and organize them into a paragraph. Finally, bring the paragraph to an end with a good concluding sentence.

Topic: _____

1. Write a Rough Outline

The Topic Sentence: _____

_____

The Supporting Ideas: _____

_____

_____

2. Write a Paragraph

_____

_____

_____

參考答案請參閱解答本 p. 16

Unit 29

Persuasive and Argumentative Writing

There are times we have different points of view and there are always pros and cons of an argument ranging from personal affairs to the national policy. For example, we may persuade a person not to take drugs, discuss the advantages and disadvantages of watching TV, insist that death penalty should be or should not be abolished or suggest that mercy killing should be legal or illegal. In these cases, the writer will manage to persuade the readers to agree with his or her argument.

In persuasive writing, the goal is to convince readers to agree with and accept a given point of view. To reach the goal, first, the writer has to choose a position: whether he or she is for or against the topic. Next, the writer has to collect and study the information related to the argument from reliable sources. For example, the writer may have to make reference to the reports and consult the experts so that he or she will be able to provide sufficient, strong, and convincing evidence to support the argument for the readers to be fully persuaded. The forms of supporting evidence may include the following:

- experiments
- facts and examples
- statistics or numerical facts
- logical or reasonable reasoning (推斷)
- reports and information from credible (可信的) sources
- emotional appeal
- studies or experts' opinions
- personal experience and ideas

📖 Example ➤

Topic: Should high school students work part time?

Arguments:

For → 1. Working part time will lessen the time for study so they will learn how to budget their time.

2. They will realize that making money is not an easy job and they

will spend money wisely.

      3. They may help support the family.

Against → 1. The duty of students is studying. If they take a part time job, they will not have enough time to study.

      2. If they make money just for themselves, they may spend more money on something unnecessary and get into the habit of luxury.

      3. They may meet people who have bad influence on them.

Exercise A

Think of an argument for and against each of the following topics.

1.

Topic: Students' academic performance should be evaluated based on written reports instead of on the results of standardized tests.

Arguments:

For → _____

_____

_____

Against → _____

_____

_____

2.

Topic: Teenagers use smartphones too often and depend on them.

Arguments:

For → _____

_____

_____

Against → _____

_____

_____

3.

Topic: Students should wear uniforms to school.

Arguments:

For → _____

_____

_____

Against → _____

_____

_____

💡 參考答案請參閱解答本 **p. 16**

Organization of a persuasive essay

Introduction: topic or argument	Present the topic. Describe the background of an argument or a problem and then clearly state your point of view. Pick the side you wish to advocate (主張), avoiding ambiguous (模稜兩可的), vague, or general statements.
Body: supporting details (one or more paragraphs)	Back up the topic sentence with evidence, arguments, or examples. • Write from both objective and subjective points of view. • Provide ideas that are convincing enough to persuade your readers to accept them. • Discuss and criticize opposing opinions point by point to create a stronger argument.
Conclusion	Briefly and strongly restate your topic and make a conclusion.

PROS & CONS

📖 Example ▶

The following is a persuasive and argumentative essay on "Mercy Killing." Read the essay and write down the outline of the essay and the supporting details for argument.

With highly advanced medical equipment and medical care and treatment, even the critically ill patients can keep alive for longer time than we can ever imagine. For example, the patients who are claimed to have little or no chance of recovery may depend on life support to live on. However, whether it is a blessing is a question and mercy killing becomes something worth discussing.

I am of the opinion that mercy killing should be done when it is time. By definition, "mercy killing" is done out of good will and kindness so it is the right thing to do. There are several reasons. So far as the patients are concerned, depending on life support, they suffer severe pain or even remain unconscious. In a way, they are not really alive. They have already passed away. Why not stop torturing them? As for the family members, they are suffering, too. They may feel tired out, depressed, or even hopeless. What's worse, if they are poor, the caring for the patients would be both a burden and a torture to them. Besides, it's a waste of social resources and manpower.

Some may insist that even if there is a chance in a million or even no chance at all, the patients should "live" on. The existence of the patient seems to give them a sense of comfort. However, it is not a matter of living or not, but a matter of dignity. It is meaningless, inhuman and cruel to force them to live on like that. Wouldn't it be better for the beloved to die with dignity than lie there unconsciously with medical equipment?

Life is precious. We must cherish every moment when we are healthy. However, when it is time, we must learn to let go and let ourselves or our beloved ones rest in peace.

Outline of the Essay

1st paragraph: (→ *the background of the argument*)

Highly advanced medical equipment and medical care and treatment keep the critically ill patients alive for longer time than we can ever imagine.

2nd and 3rd paragraphs: (→ *pros and cons of the argument*)

pros	cons
a. It is done out of good will and kindness. b. The patients remain unconscious. They are not really alive. c. It's a torture to both the patients and the family members. d. The family members feel exhausted, depressed and hopeless. e. It's a waste of social resources and manpower. f. It is meaningless, inhuman and cruel to force the patients to live on without dignity.	a. Even there is only one chance in a million, they won't give up. b. The existence of the patients gives comfort to their family members.

4th paragraph: (→ *concluding paragraph*)

We must cherish every moment when we are healthy. However, when it is time, we must learn to let go and let ourselves or our beloved ones rest in peace.

The following are some transitional words and phrases used in a persuasive paragraph or essay to help organize supporting ideas into better arguments.

1. Giving reasons or evidences:

> for example, for one thing, for another thing, to begin with, first of all, most important of all, most importantly, in fact, in general, in other words, that is, the truth is that, according to, based on, I am for/against . . . , etc.

2. Giving more evidences:

> What's more/better/worse, besides, furthermore, moreover, also, finally, in addition (to), etc.

3. Showing results or conclusion:

> as a result, therefore, consequently, in consequence, accordingly, in this way, in a word, in short, to sum up, etc.

4. Showing opposite opinions:

on the contrary, however, etc.

Exercise B

Complete the following paragraphs by using proper transitional words or phrases.

It's a good idea for the elderly to keep dogs as pets. Dogs are considered the most loyal animal. With the company of dogs, old people will feel less lonely. 1_____, dogs can be trained to take care of the elders, as often seen in newspapers and reports. 2_____, they may protect their masters and even ask for help if necessary.

3_____, being busy with their pets, old people have no time to feel lonely. They have to feed and bathe their dogs and attend to their health just like taking care of a child. They also have to walk the dog. As a result of walking the dog regularly, they will be healthier. 4_____, they are very likely to know more people, have more friends and lead a more active life.

參考答案請參閱解答本 p. 16

Exercise C

Write a persuasive essay on "Joining a school club is a good idea for high school students." Your essay should be at least 120 words in length.

_____

_____

_____

參考答案請參閱解答本 p. 16～17

Unit 30

Classification

In a classification paragraph, the writer arranges people, things, or ideas into groups based on shared characteristics. It often features examples that are organized according to types, parts, or categories.

Brainstorm

Before writing a classification paragraph, you will first need to choose a topic broad enough to be divided into groups. After you decide on your topic, it should be arranged into subgroups according to their shared characteristics.

📖 Example

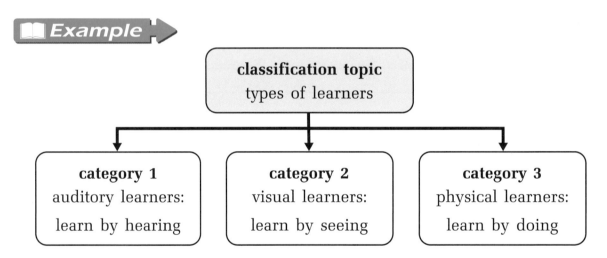

classification topic
types of learners

category 1
auditory learners:
learn by hearing

category 2
visual learners:
learn by seeing

category 3
physical learners:
learn by doing

✏ Exercise A

Fill in the following blanks by dividing writing into four categories based on their shared characteristics.

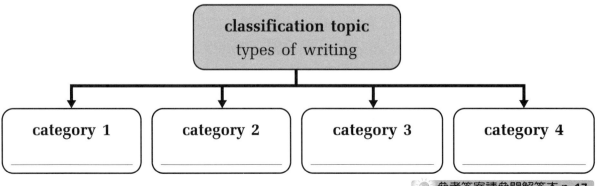

classification topic
types of writing

category 1
_____

category 2
_____

category 3
_____

category 4
_____

參考答案請參閱解答本 p. 17

Transitional words or phrases that are often used in a classification paragraph can be categorized as follows:

1. Indicating addition:

first (of all), to begin with, first, second, third, following that, after that, then, lastly, finally, etc.

2. Giving examples:

for example, for instance, etc.

Exercise B

Complete the following classification paragraph with a proper transitional word in the box below. The first one has been done for you.

~~to begin with~~   for example   second   lastly

Learners can be classified into three main types: auditory, visual, and physical, according to their different learning styles. [1]*To begin with*, there are auditory learners, who would rather listen to their learning materials than read them. They basically depend on listening to either a teacher or other forms of audio instruction to learn new things. [2]_____, there are visual learners, who learn best through graphics, demonstrations, or reading. They rely on visual aids to learn effectively. [3]_____, they may use pictures, videos, or diagrams to help them process the information. [4]_____, for physical learners, physically performing process is the way to learn. They process information through "hands-on" experience. For this kind of students, learning by doing is the easiest way for them to learn.

參考答案請參閱解答本 p. 17

The purpose of a classification paragraph is to clearly define a term or category and then to further subdivide it into groups on the basis of important differences between them.

1. **The Topic Sentence**

The topic sentence of a classification paragraph should provide an overview (概述) for the whole paragraph. It is composed of two parts: the topic and the controlling idea, which is the basis of classification. It controls how the writer deals with the subject.

Examples

· Generally speaking, abuse can **be categorized into** physical abuse, mental abuse, and sexual abuse.

· Sports shoes **are divided into** the categories of professional sports, stylish sports, and leisure sports.

· We can **classify** energy resources into two types—renewable and non-renewable.

2. **The Supporting Ideas**

In the body of the paragraph, you should describe or illustrate each subtype with key, defining details.

Here are some tips for giving supporting ideas:

(1) Supporting details should be focused on describing each category and how it relates to the broader topic.

(2) The details should be arranged in the same order as they appear in the topic sentence. The most important category can be saved for last.

(3) You should provide the same quantity and give the same number of examples for each category.

(4) To connect the categories, be sure to use proper transitional words or phrases.

3. **The Concluding Sentence**

At the end of the paragraph, add a closing sentence to provide a general summary statement about the subject.

Exercise C

Give each of the following paragraphs an appropriate topic sentence.

1. _____

_____ The main concern of price shoppers is the cost of goods. These shoppers usually have a tight budget, so they usually shop at discount stores. As for value shoppers, they usually have no financial problems, and what they care most is the value of goods. They don't mind paying more for better quality or extra service. When it comes to luxury shoppers, all they want is the best. They are usually well-off; thus, they are willing to pay everything for luxurious goods and the best service. What kind of shoppers are you?

2. _____

_____ Of the above three methods, regular exercise is the healthiest. Whether you go to a gym, work out at home, take part in an exercise class, or play on a sports team, it not only keeps you in good shape but helps you stay healthy. The second best way to lose weight is through calorie control. By carefully calculating and limiting the calories

 you take in every day, you can reach your ideal weight without affecting your health. Lastly, having surgery such as having a band put around the stomach, is also an effective way to get rid of excess weight. Most of the people who have undergone this operation lose 50% of their excess weight in the first two years after surgery.

參考答案請參閱解答本 p. 17

Exercise D

Write a classification paragraph for the topic sentence "Scientists have categorized volcanoes into three main categories: active, dormant (休眠的), and extinct."

參考答案請參閱解答本 p. 17

Summary

A summary is a piece of writing that gives the main points of a text rather than its details. There are times we must make a summary. For example, we are asked to describe a journey, a story, to restate a report or studies, or to explain a happening. The focus should be on the main points. A good summary must be short, complete, and faithful to the original text without duplicating (複製) any part of it. Therefore, it is suggested that the main ideas should be paraphrased instead of simply being copied from the original text. Besides, a summary should never include any of your own ideas or opinions.

Below are the steps toward writing an effective summary.

1. Before writing, first, read the article carefully to get a clear picture of what the article is about. Then, mark or take notes of the key points.

2. Based on the notes, write an outline including introduction, body and conclusion.

3. Write down the main idea of each paragraph or each section.

4. Provide each main idea with supporting ideas.

5. After writing the summary, read your summary, check out the main idea and supporting ideas. Modify where it is necessary. Be sure of the fluency of the summary and correct spelling.

The following are some tips for writing a summary.

1. Instead of copying the original, write in your own words.

2. Be sure to include the main ideas and supporting points but avoid minor details.

3. Be faithful to the original. Don't include anything that is not mentioned in the original.

4. Don't involve personal opinions or comments.

📖 Example ▶

Read the following essay, and make a summary of it in no more than 200 words.

Volunteers have long played an important role in our lives. They are enthusiastic people who simply like to help others and never ask for payment. The concept of "volunteering" began centuries ago. In the early American colonies, people were expected to spend their spare time helping out in their communities. Benjamin Franklin, one of the most influential politicians in American history, put this idea into practice by setting up a volunteer fire department in Philadelphia. Today, most rural communities and many small towns in the U.S.A. still depend on volunteers to fight fires.

In modern society, volunteer work remains as important as it has ever been. In fact, more and more people are taking part in volunteer work. For example, they take scout groups on camping trips, clean up town parks, and pick up litter along hiking trails. What's more, they also visit the sick and the elderly to provide them with care and help.

It is obvious that volunteer work helps society. However, does it also help the volunteers? Do volunteers get anything out of their work, besides the sense of achievement? Sure they do. Through volunteer work, most people can get valuable experience and knowledge. Many volunteers can also learn new skills which prepare them for full-time jobs. Moreover, it might surprise you that such experience is sometimes as helpful as a degree when it comes to landing a job. Let us say you sort mail in the office of a hospital on weekdays. When the weekend comes, it is time for you, the volunteer, to go out and raise funds on the busy city streets or in front of shopping centers. Now, it may seem worthless to do all of this unpaid work. But when you are looking for a paid job, the experience you've gained as a volunteer may give you an advantage over other job seekers. That is, job seekers with volunteer experience are more likely to be hired than those people who have never volunteered. The reason is that they have had more chances to learn how to handle difficulties.

Of course, volunteer work may have nothing to do with the career you want to pursue. Does that mean there's no benefit in it? Absolutely not! Volunteer work can teach you a lot about yourself—and this is probably the greatest benefit of all. Volunteer work can help you explore what you are able to do best. In addition, it can help you learn about certain kinds of work and the way to deal with other people as well.

Your future is important, and your service to society is important, too. Have you ever volunteered? If you haven't, it's time for you to get involved in such unpaid work!

Steps

1. Read and get the general information: It's about volunteer work.
2. Write down the topic of each paragraph and supporting points.
   (1) What's the definition of "volunteer work" and its origin?
   (2) What can volunteers do to help the society?
   (3) What advantages do volunteers get out of their volunteer work?
   (4) Volunteer work helps people in many ways.
   (5) Get involved in volunteer work and serve the society.
3. Write a draft based on the topic of each paragraph without including the details.
4. Check out, make changes and make sure of no misspelling.

The summary

Volunteers are enthusiastic people. They are ready to help without asking anything in return. Since long time ago, volunteers have played an important part in the society. Now, there are more and more volunteers. They do almost everything from cleaning up parks to visiting the sick and the elderly to provide them with care and help.

Besides the sense of achievement, volunteers can get valuable experience and knowledge. They can also learn new skills. When it is necessary, the experience they've gained as a volunteer may give them an advantage over others. Besides, they have had more chances to learn how to handle difficulties.

Most importantly, volunteer work can teach them a lot about

themselves. It can help them explore what they are able to do best. Besides, it helps them learn about different kinds of work and the way to deal with other people.

All in all, a volunteer's service benefits the society and the volunteers themselves, too.

Exercise A

You must have heard the story "The Boy Who Cried Wolf" from "Aesop's Fables." Write a summary of the story in less than 150 words.

> 參考答案請參閱解答本 p. 17

Exercise B

The following is the origin of the Dragon Boat Festival. Write a summary of it in no more than 150 words.

The Dragon Boat Festival, also called Double Fifth Festival, is celebrated on the fifth day of the fifth month of the lunar calendar.

The Chinese Dragon Boat Festival is an important holiday celebrated in China. It is one of the most important Chinese festivals and the other two significant festivals are the Autumn Moon Festival and Chinese New Year.

The origin of Dragon Boat Festival centers around a scholarly government official named Chu Yuan. He was a good and respected man, but because of the misdeeds of jealous rivals, he eventually fell into disfavor in the emperor's court. Unable to regain the respect of the emperor, in his sadness Chu Yuan threw himself into the Mi Lo River.

Because of their admiration for Chu Yuan, the local people living nearby the Mi Lo River rushed into their boats to search for him and threw rice wrapped with bamboo leaves into the waters. They hoped that the fish in the river would eat the rice they threw instead of the body of Chu Yuan. Although they were unable to find Chu Yuan's body, their efforts are still commemorated today during the Dragon Boat Festival.

Because of this, now it has become a tradition for people to have rice dumplings on Dragon Boat Festival. In addition, the celebration is also a time for protection from evil and disease for the rest of the year. It is done by different practices such as hanging healthy herbs on the front door, drinking Hsiunghuang, which is a kind of alcohol, and displaying portraits of evils nemesis (勁敵), Chung Kuei. By doing these, people hope that everything will go well in the year.

參考答案請參閱解答本 p. 17

Autobiography

An autobiography is about a person's life written by the person himself/herself. Writing an autobiography is a way of telling people about your life: who you are, what you have done, and what you hope to achieve. An autobiography may be written either for general purposes or for a specific purpose. The former is about giving a brief introduction of oneself. The latter is written for specific purposes such as applying for a position or to a school. Regardless of its purpose, what matters is not how much detailed information you include, but how impressive and persuasive it is.

Below are the steps toward writing an effective autobiography.

1. Outline your family and education background, and then explain how they have influenced you.

2. Talk about your personality traits, abilities, special skills, and interests. Also, mention any prizes or recognition you've earned, the activities you've taken part in, and any formal academic or technical qualifications you've got. Be sure to stay focused on what is related to your purpose in writing the autobiography. For example, if you are writing an autobiography for asking admission to a school, you have to prove that you are interested in the subject that you would like to major in and that you are qualified for being admitted. If you apply for a position, it will be important to prove that you are competent enough and that you deserve the job. Therefore, you have to prove that you are knowledgeable, professional and experienced to convince others of your qualification and competence.

3. Describe what you will do if you are admitted to the school or get the job, what your ultimate goals are and how you intend to reach them.

The following are some tips for writing an autobiography.

1. Make the autobiography simple and easy to understand.

2. Show yourself and your abilities in a positive attitude.

3. Add color to your autobiography but never lie, boast, or exaggerate.

4. After finishing your autobiography, check it out and be absolutely certain that there are no grammatical errors or misspelling (拼錯) at all.

📖 Example

Read the following autobiography of a poor Indian boy Sandeep Shahani, the boy in the documentary "Children of the World." and write down the organization of his autobiography.

My name is Sandeep Shahani. I am twelve years old. I was born into a poor family in India. My father is a boatman, and he rows people across the river every day. He works around the clock, earning little money to support my family.

My family name "Shahani" literally means "boatman." That is, based on the caste system in India, this is the career I was born into. It seems that I am destined to follow in my father's footsteps, always staying in my hometown and living a hard life without any chance of changing my life.

Since I am only a young boy, there is little I can do. However, I do wish that my life were not so confined by the class I belong to. I want to see the world and do something different. When I grow older, I will definitely make every effort to improve myself and aim at helping people out of inequality and mistreatment. I will never stop working hard until I achieve my dream.

Organization of Sandeep Shahani's autobiography

	Main idea	**Details**
1st paragraph	the introduction and background of the writer's family	1. He is twelve years old. 2. He was born into a poor family. 3. His father is a boat man, working around the clock, earning very little money.
2nd paragraph	the meaning of his family name and what he thinks about his future	1. "Shahani" means "boatman." 2. Based on the caste system in India, he is destined to follow in my father's footsteps. 3. He has to stay in his hometown and live a hard life without any chance of changing his life.

		1. As a young boy, he can't do anything.
3rd paragraph	what he expects of his future, his dream and what he will do	2. He wishes that his life were not confined by the class he belongs to. 3. He wants to see the world and do something different. 4. When he grows older, he will definitely make every effort to improve himself and aim at helping people out of inequality and mistreatment. 5. He will never stop working hard until he achieves his dream.

Exercise A

According to the following information, write an autobiography from the 1st person perspective. Your essay should be more than 120 words in length.

Name: Andrew Carnegie, once the world's richest person, born in 1835 and died in 1919.

Family background:

1. His father was a rich weaver. He was expected to follow his father's profession.
2. The Industrial Revolution destroyed the weaver's craft.
3. His family moved to Pittsburgh, U.S.A., the iron-manufacturing center of the country.

His working experience:

1. He took odd jobs at a cotton factory.
2. He worked as a messenger boy in the telegraph office.
3. He delivered messages to the city theater.
4. He spent most of his leisure hours in a small library available for working boys.
5. He made a large fortune. (After the civil war, he was devoted to replacing wooden bridges with iron ones. He introduced a new refining process to convert iron into steel. By 1900, Carnegie Steel produced more of the metal than all of Great Britain.)

His attitudes towards his business:

1. He often expressed uneasiness with his business life.

2. He wished to spend more time receiving instruction and reading systematically.

3. He considered it a disgrace to put most of the thoughts on making money.

4. He sold his company and retired at 64.

After retirement:

1. He said, "The man who dies rich dies disgraced."

2. He gave away his fortune. (He established over 2500 public libraries, sponsored numerous cultural, educational and scientific institutions. He had given away 350 million dollars.)

參考答案請參閱解答本 p. 17～18

Write your own autobiography which is meant for applying to a college. Your essay should be more than 120 words in length.

Outline of the autobiography

1st paragraph: name, the school you are studying in, family background

2nd paragraph: your interests, the activities, clubs and competitions you attended regarding the subject you are applying for

3rd paragraph: future plans after entering the college and after graduating from college

參考答案請參閱解答本 p. 18

Study Plan

When applying to a college, you may be required to submit a plan of study. Before you begin, think about your interests and do some research into the courses offered at the university you are applying to. In the first part of your study plan, briefly mention your reasons for choosing to study at this university and show the school that you are familiar with the courses they offer. Then, divide your plan into short-term, mid-term, and long-term goals. After discussing each set of goals, conclude your study plan by restating your eagerness to enter the university.

Example

Imagine that you are applying to a psychology department. Write a rough outline for your study plan first, and then develop your ideas into an essay.

Introduction	desire to make a difference in people's lives, course offerings	
Body: Study Plan	Short-term Goal	do extensive reading, improve language skills, do volunteer work
	Mid-term Goal	take required and elective courses
	Long-term Goal	create and apply new theories to psychology
Conclusion	emphasize passion and ambition	

Since I am a person who enjoys helping others, my classmates and friends often pour out their hearts to me. Instead of getting impatient with them, I listen attentively and try to help them deal with whatever problems they are facing. As a result of this, I have become interested in counseling and learning how to analyze other people's problems and guide them toward a solution.

According to the information I've gathered, your undergraduate program has three main focuses: cognitive psychology, developmental psychology, and social psychology. The emphasis placed on students' research in all of these areas is what attracts me the most. I hope that

someday the results of my research can advance knowledge in this field and benefit society. My goals are as follows:

Short-term Goal (from now to the beginning of classes)

During the five months before the semester starts, I will do my best to read extensively. I will read not only books on basic psychology but also other good books that I did not have time to read in high school. Moreover, I intend to improve my English proficiency by reading English novels and watching English movies so that I will not be intimidated by textbooks in English later.

Mid-term Goal (four years in college)

After finishing my required courses, I want to focus more on sociology and related fields. At the same time, I would like to take courses in research methodology as well. Thus, most of my time will be devoted to doing research, attending professional conferences and presenting research findings.

Long-term Goal (after graduation)

Since I am interested in pursuing advanced studies after college, I plan to apply to graduate school to concentrate on a specific area of research and play a more active role in the field. After graduation, my goal is to teach and do research in a university, making a contribution both to my field and to society.

If I am lucky enough to be admitted to your department, I will dedicate myself to the study of psychology in the hope of one day being a successful researcher.

Exercise

I. *Write a rough outline for your own study plan.*

Introduction		
Body: Study Plan	Short-term Goal	
	Mid-term Goal	
	Long-term Goal	
Conclusion		

II. *Based on the outline above, develop your ideas into an essay.*

参考答案請參閱解答本 p. 18～19

掌握關鍵，瞄準致勝！

學測指考英文
致勝句型

王隆興／編著

致勝關鍵

關鍵1 名師嚴選80個句型重點！

完整收錄大考常見句型，並比較易混淆的句型，清楚掌握重點，舉一反三。

關鍵2 解說清楚明瞭一看就懂！

重點一目瞭然，說明淺顯易懂好吸收，考前衝刺神隊友，迅速提升考場即戰力。

關鍵3 隨堂評量實戰練習現學現用！

隨書附贈20回隨堂評量，及時檢視學習成果、熟悉句型，以收事半功倍之效。

英文中級字彙王

丁雍嫻、邢雯桂、盧思嘉、應惠蕙／編著

★ 符合最新學測範圍，收錄學測必考高頻率單字，讓學生掌握學測所需字彙力。

★ 單字搭配精心編寫例句、常用介系詞和重要片語詳列，讓學生完全掌握單字用法。

★ 同反義字補充豐富，讓學生輕鬆延伸學習範圍。

★ 全書共 100 回：Level 3 共 40 回，Level4 共 40 回，Level 5 共 20 回。

★ 每回附練習題，題型豐富，讓學生即時驗收學習成效。

★ 附免費 APP，手機 APP 在手，學測字彙帶著走。

作文100隨身讀

三民英語編輯小組　彙整
三民／東大英文教材主編 車畇庭　審定

作文100，
大考英文作文的搶分祕笈！

★ 一手掌握，作文必勝：
　　口袋書型式，大小適中，讓你隨時隨地都能加強作文。
★ 分類彙整，篇篇實用：
　　全書共100篇作文範例，共分為3大部分：看圖寫作、信函寫作和主題寫作。
★ 取材廣泛，主題豐富：
　　不僅蒐羅近年學測、指考及各校模擬考試作文題目，還提供各式主題範文。
★ 單字片語，學以致用：
　　詳列重要單字片語，讓你一邊學作文，一邊累積字彙。
★ 寫作技巧，指點迷津：
　　提供精闢的寫作建議，教你如何下筆，讓你考試臨場發揮自如。

學科能力測驗、指定科目考試、全民英檢中級/中高級適用
亦可搭配十二年國教課綱加深加廣選修課程「英文作文」

英語 *Make Me High* 系列

WRITE RIGHT, NO NG

英文這樣寫，不NG

解答本

三民書局

Unit 1

Exercise A

What kind	The **colorful wild** bird flew.
How	The colorful wild bird flew **fast**.
Where	The colorful wild bird flew fast **in the sky**.
When	The colorful wild bird flew fast in the sky **this afternoon**.
Why	The colorful wild bird flew fast in the sky this afternoon **because it was looking for food**.

Exercise B

1. On the hall walls, Jack saw many sports medals and some pictures of students.
2. Do you want to meet me in the cafeteria for lunch or play basketball with me after school?
3. I'd be glad to play basketball with you, but it must be after school.

Exercise C

2. Peter, one of my close friends, lives next to my grandmother.
3. I can totally understand your feelings because I was a new student as well last year.
4. I discovered an envelope inside the bag after I had eaten several cookies.

Exercise D

I. 2. crept   3. letter

II.

old; warmly; slowly; quietly; luxurious; young; rich; iced; poor; comfortable

III.

1. The thief crept.
   → The thief crept slowly and quietly.
2. The man wrote a letter.
   → The tall man carefully wrote a letter.

IV.

on; under; near; in; at; between; across; in front of; to; outward

V.

1. The thief crept slowly and quietly into the house.
   → The thief crept slowly and quietly into the rich man's luxurious house.
2. The tall man carefully wrote a letter.
   → The tall man carefully wrote a letter to his friend.

VI.

and; until; when; before; after; because; as; since; although; if

VII.

1. The thief crept slowly and quietly to the rich man's luxurious house.
   → When it was completely dark, the thief crept slowly and quietly to the rich man's luxurious house.
2. The tall man carefully wrote a letter to his friend.
   → The tall man carefully wrote a letter of apology to his friend and put it in a plain envelope.

Unit 2

2-1 Exercise

2-2 Exercise

Topic: Food

Ideas:

· I like sashimi
· Green vegetables are good for you
· I usually have some dessert after dinner
· Fast food is bad for one's health
· Some foreign dishes look scary, such as roast snail and fried bees

Unit 3

Exercise A

2. Topic: Exercise

The controlling idea: good for your health

3. Topic: Make friends

The controlling idea: is like making soup

Exercise B

2. Colors do spice up ordinary conversations.

3. Mr. Nelson is the teacher that changed my life.

4. Baseball is a sport that most people in Taiwan like.

5. Global warming (全球暖化) has greatly changed the earth's climate.

Exercise C

1. We should always tell the truth.

2. Here are some easy tips for you to learn how to enjoy opera.

Exercise D

1. Different colors are used for different purposes.

2. Having a group of close friends helps bring together those who can do different things.

Unit 4

Exercise A

1. C   2. A   3. D

Exercise B

B.

Topic sentence: International trade is the exchange of goods and services between countries.

Supporting idea 1: sentence 2

Supporting idea 2: sentence 3

Supporting idea 3: sentence 4

C.

Topic sentence: Many patients have reported a decrease in pain after a good laugh.

Supporting idea 1: sentence 2

Supporting idea 2: sentence 3 (The patients' muscles are more relaxed.)

Supporting idea 3: sentence 3 (The patients are distracted from thinking about their pain.)

Exercise C

1.

(A) The food is ready in a short time.

(B) The place is usually big and clean.

(C) It's pretty easy to find a fast-food restaurant in most cities.

2.

(A) Quite a few young couples choose to have only one child or no child at all.

(B) Some couples can't afford to raise any child.

(C) More and more people would prefer to be single.

Unit 5

Exercise A

1. B   2. D   3. A

Exercise B

1. Clearly, from a young age, we learn about the importance of honesty.

2. Though people are unable to predict the future, they still try their best to find a way to control it.

3. If we make good use of television, it can play an important part in children education.

4. Thus, it is not surprising that so many men and women have trouble communicating with each other.

5. My high school life becomes richer because of this experience.

Unit 6

Exercise A

2. All in all   3. Therefore   4. In fact   5. that is

6. In other words

Exercise B

1. for example   2. thus   3. However

Exercise C

1. C   2. A   3. D   4. F   5. B

Exercise D

1. *As a result*, the government decided to send a unit of soldiers to help the locals.

2. *Besides*, I can surf the internet for information. *Most important of all*, my cell phone is also a

dictionary. *All in all*, my cell phone is a necessity for me.

3. *In addition*, through volunteer work, she gains valuable job experience. *Best of all*, volunteering helps her realize what she is able to do best and helps her learn how to deal with other people as well.

Unit 7

Exercise

2. ;.   3. ",", 4. ;, 5. ,! 6. ;,;. 7. — 8. :,,,.
9. ;—. 10. ,,

Unit 8

Exercise A

2. the; the; a; × 3. ×; × 4. an; ×

Exercise B

2. C 3. F 4. A 5. D 6. G 7. B

Exercise C

1. the 2. Either 3. a 4. Neither 5. every
6. every; much

Unit 9

Exercise

2. own 3. were 4. have 5. were 6. like 7. is
8. is 9. knows 10. was 11. were 12. wear
13. suffer 14. is; is; are 15. were; took 16. are
17. has 18. is 19. is 20. was

Unit 10

Exercise A

2. his or her 3. themselves; they 4. you; you
5. them

Exercise B

I. 2. he 3. him 4. I 5. him
II. 1. you 2. your 3. you 4. their 5. them

Unit 11

Exercise A

2. taught 3. stays 4. stole 5. are

Exercise B

2. would 3. were 4. heard 5. have

Exercise C

I.

2. needed 3. got 4. was 5. stopped 6. thought
7. Is 8. was 9. am 10. is

II.

1. was 2. was 3. means 4. picked 5. would

Unit 12

Exercise A

2. C 3. F 4. F 5. C

Exercise B

2. C

There is a sharp contrast between the poor and the rich. The poor may have to worry about their next meal while the rich may spend thousands or even tens of thousands on a handbag.

3. A

There are advantages of getting into the habit of taking notes. Whether you are reading, studying or listening to a speech, it is useful to write down the information you may want to look up later. In the process of writing down what is mentioned, you are actually organizing information at the same time.

4. A

The Annals of Improbable Research is an American magazine that celebrates the funny side of science. Each year, ten winners are awarded prizes. Most of the award-winning research may seem unusual, but it usually grabs people's attention instead. And no matter how ridiculous the research sounds, people can find it inspiring and amusing.

5. C

There are several reasons I need to find a roommate. He or she can share the rent. Besides, I have someone to talk to. Most importantly, the room would be more like "home" instead of a place to live.

Unit 13

Exercise A

2. The press has a strong influence; it can bring about significant changes to the lives of ordinary people.

3. Hsu made this film to indicate that global warming had already become quite serious (,) and she hoped that her film could help focus public attention on environmental protection.

4. Small islands and low coastal areas could soon be underwater; the residents of major cities are likely to have nowhere to live by the end of the 21st century.

5. It was very hard to find a job; more than one hundred applicants were interviewed for five vacancies.

Exercise B

2. Even though you fail a test, you don't have to feel frustrated. On the contrary, you should study even harder.

3. A man can stay alive for more than a week without food. However, a man without water can hardly live for more than three days.

4. When/After my mom heard what I said, she stepped out of my room without saying a word.

5. Robert is enthusiastic and kind-hearted because he works as a volunteer in the hospital. Besides, he donates money to the orphanage regularly.

Unit 14

Exercise

1.

A miser hid all of his money in a hole and put a heavy stone to the top. One day, he lifted the stone but found no penny there. He cried so loudly that his neighbors came running to see what was happening. One of the neighbors told him that he didn't need to be unhappy at all since he never thought of how to do with the money.

2.

In many languages, certain animals have specific characteristics. In Chinese, for example, dogs represent loyalty, and lions are the symbol of authority. Likewise, animal imagery can be found in many English expressions. "As busy as a bee" and "as quiet as a mouse" vividly describe a busy person and a quiet person. The imagery gives color to the language.

3.

The pronunciation of the word for "pineapple" in Taiwanese means "prosperity or good luck will come." Naturally, it has become a symbol of wealth in Chinese culture. Thus, it is common to find pineapples placed in houses during Chinese New Year. Baozi is another instance. The word "baozi," together with the word "zongzi," sounds like "a sure victory." No wonder, Chinese people give "baozi" together with "zongzi" to the examinees to wish them a sure victory.

Unit 15

15-1 Exercise

2. FN   3. TN   4. TN   5. FN

15-2 Exercise

A. Finally   B. then   C. One day   D. from then on
E. After   F. before   H. When   I. then
The correct order is:
C → G → E → I → A → H → F → B → D

15-3 Exercise

1.

1. got up late on a school day
2. fell down because the sidewalk was too slippery
3. got wet because I didn't have an umbrella with me
4. my glasses broke
5. muddy water splashed all over me
6. my classmates laughed at me
7. missed the bus

↓

Group A:

1. got up late on a school day

3. got wet because I didn't have an umbrella with me

7. missed the bus

Group B:

2. fell down because the sidewalk was too slippery

4. my glasses broke

5. muddy water splashed all over me

Group C:

6. my classmates laughed at me

2.

The Topic Sentence: I had a very bad day yesterday

The Supporting Ideas:

① Group A: overslept and forgot my umbrella

② Group B: slipped on the sidewalk and broke my glasses

③ Group C: was teased by my classmates

3.

    I had a very bad morning yesterday. To begin with, I overslept and missed my bus. Then, as I rushed out of the door, it started to rain. I didn't want to waste any time running back home to get an umbrella, so I simply put my schoolbag under my jacket, hoping that it wouldn't get too wet. But then suddenly, I slipped and fell on the wet sidewalk. My glasses flew off, and everyone started looking at me. I was very embarrassed. But my bad morning didn't end there. As I was trying to find my glasses, a car drove through a puddle of water and splashed water all over me. It was very hard for me to see anything with my face covered with muddy water. I finally found my glasses, but they were broken. Wet and dirty from head to toe, I finally arrived at school. When my classmates saw me, they all broke out into laughter. It goes without saying that yesterday really was not my day.

Unit 16

16-1 Exercise

    It was a warm day in spring. The sky was blue and the cloud was white. Jim decided to go out for a walk with his puppy dog. They went to the park in his community. Walking through the park, Jim wanted to have a rest so he sat under the big, tall tree. He bent his arms behind his head and watched what people were doing in the park. He noticed that there was an old couple sitting on the bench. The old man and the old woman enjoyed the breeze and wore smiles on their faces. In the blue sky were some birds singing happily. A cute cat was sitting quietly on the garbage can. Suddenly, Jim heard a cry out of surprise. It was the girl who made this sound. The girl in the dress was standing in front of the drinking fountain. She was so surprised to find the water coming out of the facility. Jim recalled his childhood because he did the same thing as the curious girl when he was five years old.

16-2 Exercise

    Jenny and Jared are twins and they received brand new iPhones as their birthday gifts from their parents yesterday. They were thrilled to get the fancy presents. Jenny was fascinated by the multiple functions the iPhone had and thus became a phubber (低頭族) since she couldn't take her eyes off the screen. On the other hand, Jared had already mastered the smartphone's functions and indulged in the tracks he had downloaded from iTunes.

    This morning, the twins walked to school with their iPhones. Jenny fixed her eyes on her smartphone again while Jared was happily enjoying the top songs on the billboard. Their mother and young sister followed behind them to keep them company. All of a sudden, Jenny hit a tree trunk because she paid no attention to the road ahead. So strong was the impact that she almost passed out. Jenny's mother came to her aid immediately, blaming her for not concentrating. Meanwhile, Jared was still listening to music with his eyes closed. Not noticing what was going on, he kept walking as if the outside world didn't exist.

While crossing the road, Jared was still wearing his headphones. The volume he set was too high for him to hear other sounds. Little did he know that he had blocked the way of a few cars. At that time, a furious man suddenly appeared in front of him and pulled his headphones off. "Pay attention to traffic safety, dude," shouted the man as he pointed behind. Jared was shocked to see that there was a heavy traffic jam. He apologized and walked across the street quickly engulfed in flames of embarrassment.

Before long, Jared saw his family on the sidewalk and surprisingly found Jenny had a bruise on her forehead. Annoyed with the twins, their mother decided to take back their iPhones until they learned the importance of safety. Staring at each other, Jenny and Jared exchanged a knowing look. They would keep today's lesson in mind forever. (改編自學測佳作)

Unit 17

17-1 Exercise

1.

---
1. Jack likes to wear black T-shirts and old jeans
2. Jack is interested in computers
3. Jack has straight, green hair
4. Jack's knowledge of computers is second to none
5. Jack is tall

↓

Group A:
1. Jack likes to wear black T-shirts and old jeans
3. Jack has straight, green hair
5. Jack is tall
Group B:
2. Jack is interested in computers
4. Jack's knowledge of computers is second to none

2.
The Topic Sentence: My best friend, Jack, really lives his life in his own way.
The Supporting Ideas:
① Group A: his looks and style
② Group B: his knowledge of computers
3.

My best friend, Jack, really lives his life in his own way. He is a tall guy with straight hair that is dyed green. He usually wears black T-shirts and a pair of old blue jeans that are torn at the knees. To many people these clothes make him look a little sloppy, but he doesn't care. He believes that his style suits him well. Also, Jack claims that his knowledge of computers is second to none. He always begins our conversations by excitedly telling me interesting things he found when he was writing the programs or fixing the computers. While most of us are busy preparing for the college entrance exams, Jack has devoted himself to cyberspace and saved all of his money, in order to upgrade his computer. Unwilling to be an ordinary, obedient or average student, Jack insists on living his life in his own way.

17-2 Exercise

1.

---
1. on the east coast of Taiwan
2. the Central Cross-Island Highway
3. the red suspension bridge and the temples
4. the Eternal Spring Shrine
5. a marble canyon
6. a damp cave behind the Eternal Spring Shrine
7. eroded valleys outside the cave
8. Liwu River (立霧溪) carves away at the gorge's stone

↓

Group A:
1. on the east coast of Taiwan
Group B:
5. a marble canyon
6. a damp cave behind the Eternal Spring Shrine
---

7. eroded valleys outside the cave

8. Liwu River carves away at the gorge's stone

Group C:

2. the Central Cross-Island Highway

3. the red suspension bridge and the temples

4. the Eternal Spring Shrine

2.

The Topic Sentence: Last year I took an unforgettable trip with my family to Taroko Gorge.

The Supporting Ideas:

① Group A: location

② Group B: the natural features

③ Group C: the man-made features

3.

Last year I took an unforgettable trip with my family to Taroko Gorge, a gorgeous scenic spot on the east coast of Taiwan. One of Taiwan's main tourist attractions, Taroko Gorge is a marble canyon famous for its high-rising cliffs, deep river valleys, and uniquely shaped rocks. Following the hiking trails, my family and I went to see the red suspension bridge and the temples set in the mountains. We also visited the Eternal Spring Shrine, which is built over a waterfall and dedicated to the people who sacrificed their lives when building the Central Cross-Island Highway, which runs through Central Mountain Range and Taroko Gorge. In the back of the shrine, there are stairs leading to a cave. When I entered the cave, the damp smell of the cave hit my nostrils. It was so quiet that I could hear nothing but my own breathing. Immersed in the mysterious atmosphere in this cave, I could not stop staring at the beautiful rock formations there. Coming out of the cave, I saw magnificent mountains towering above the deep valleys. As I thought about the enormous power of the Liwu River carving on the gorge, I knew that this river and the untouched natural treasures of Taroko Gorge would always shine brightly in my mind.

17-3 Exercise

1.

1. a cotton dress shirt

2. a pleated skirt or loose-fitting pants

3. must be worn all the time except for PE class

4. a sense of school unity and spirit

5. a navy blue wool coat

6. a sense of belonging

↓

Group A:

3. must be worn all the time except for PE class

Group B:

1. a cotton dress shirt

2. a pleated skirt or loose-fitting pants

5. a navy blue wool coat

Group C:

4. a sense of school unity and spirit

6. a sense of belonging

2.

The Topic Sentence: A white shirt and black skirt or pants are the clothes that students attending our school are required to wear.

The Supporting Ideas:

① Group A: when it is worn

② Group B: how it looks and what it is made of

③ Group C: what it means to me

3.

A white shirt and black skirt or pants are the clothes that students attending our school are required to wear. Except for PE class, this uniform must be worn all the time. Worn by students on a daily basis, the uniform consists of a cotton dress shirt (short-sleeved for the summer and long-sleeved for the winter) and a pleated skirt or loose-fitting pants. Some students who don't consider it fashionable enough wear more stylish tailor-made skirts or pants. In winter, students have to wear a navy blue wool coat. To me, these uniforms create a sense of school unity and spirit. In a white shirt and black skirt or pants, everyone looks the same, thus bringing the school together. Whether the uniform looks plain or fashionable, it gives me a sense of belonging and makes me proud of being a part of my school.

Unit 18

18-1 Exercise A

	Salutation	Complimentary close
Formal letters	Dear Sirs: Dear Mrs. Lin: To whom it may concern:	Sincerely yours, Sincerely, Respectfully,
Informal letters	Hi Jack, Dear sister, My dear friend,	Love, Your daughter, Best wishes,

18-1 Exercise B

No. 101, Sec. 2, Kuang Fu Rd.,
Hsinchu City, Taiwan 30013

November 25, 2016

Ms. Emma Liu
Director of Foreign Language Department
San Min Book Co., Ltd.
8F., No. 386, Fuxing North Rd.,
Zhongshan Dist., Taipei City 10476

Dear Ms. Liu:

XXXXXXXXXXXXXXXXXXXXXXXXXXXXX
XXXXXXX

Sincerely Yours,
Jack Hong
Jack Hong

18-1 Exercise C

Aug. 12, 2016
Dear Lily,

XXXXXXXXXXXXXXXXXXXXXXXXXXXXX

Regards,
John

18-1 Exercise D

Jack Hong
No. 101, Sec. 2, Kuang Fu Rd.,
Hsinchu City, Taiwan 30013

stamp

Ms. Amy Liu
San Min Book Co., Ltd.
8F., No. 386, Fuxing North Rd.,
Zhongshan Dist., Taipei City 10476

18-2
I. Exercise

No. 28, Xinzhan Rd.,
Banqiao Dist., New Taipei City 22041
May 5, 2016

Sales Manager
Twinkle Department Store
No. 386, Fushing North Rd.,
Zhongshan Dist., Taipei City 10476

Dear Sir or Madam,

Yesterday I went to your clearance sale and made a purchase of a polka-dot dress. However, when I arrived home and opened the bag, I found a big stain right in the breast of the dress. However, when I went back to the original department to make an exchange, to my surprise, the clerk told me that no refunds for sale goods.

I really don't understand how this could happen: First, I went all the way from my home back to your store to try to settle this matter. Second, that item was clearly from your department. Third, I demanded a refund because that dress was out of stock. Finally, and most important, the mistake was not mine.

I am writing this letter to request that you make up for this mistake and to ensure such errors do not happen again. I would appreciate it if you could write or call me at (02)3683-5711 at your earliest convenience. I look forward to hearing from you soon.

Yours sincerely,
Jane Wang
Jane Wang

III. Exercise

You are cordially invited to our class reunion
Who: Class 314 of 2015
When: December 3rd, 2016, 11:00 a.m.
Where: The café near our junior high school
Why: To meet old friends and catch up on what's new with everyone

RSVP by November 20th, 2016, to Dennis at 0933-888-666.
Come and reminisce with Class 314 of 2015.

IV. Exercise A

1. It was all my fault.
2. I shouldn't have been so careless.
3. How rude of me to say that to you.
4. Please forgive me. I will never make the same mistake.

IV. Exercise B

	The reason or excuse	The way to make up for it
1.	I totally forgot about it.	Let me treat you to a movie.
2.	I had a bad cold.	I'll buy you your favorite chocolate cake.
3.	I had to prepare for my exam.	I'll walk your dog for a week for you.

IV. Exercise C

Dec. 10, 2016

Dear Joseph,

Thank you for lending me your camera. I took it with me on the trip to Green Island, but when I arrived at the hostel I was going to stay in, I was shocked to find that it was gone. I looked everywhere for it but it was no use. I wondered if I had left it on the airplane so I called the lost-and-found at the airport, but they said nobody had turned in a camera. I'm deeply sorry about this, and I have really felt bad over the last few days.

Joseph, let me buy you a new camera exactly the same as the one I lost. I'd like to treat you to dinner as well. What do you think? Please tell me when you are available and please forgive me for my carelessness.

Regretfully,
Helen

V. Exercise A

2. How nice of you to remember my birthday!
3. I would like to express my appreciation for your advice, Ms. Liu.
4. It was very nice/thoughtful/kind of you to give me a Christmas gift.

V. Exercise B

July 25, 2016

Dear Aunt Carol,

I was really excited when I received your gift. I had wanted a smartphone for a long time but I never dreamed that I could get one so soon. Aunt

Carol, thank you ever so much!

I used to envy my classmates with smartphones. They could check information anytime. They could chat and exchange ideas online anytime. When they were working on English assignments, they used their smartphones as dictionaries. Now, I can do the same. It will help me a lot both in daily life and in my schoolwork. I promise to take care of it and make the best use of it.

It's been a long time since I visited you. When the monthly examination is over, I'll come visit you and Uncle Hugh. Thank you once again for the wonderful gift.

Your nephew,
Nathan

Unit 19

Exercise A

· Venn Diagram

1. convenience 2. job opportunities 3. pollution	Places to live	1. fewer people and less traffic 2. getting close to nature and lots of fresh air 3. quiet

· Chart

	Subject A: Living in a City	Subject B: Living in the Country
feature 1: advantages	mass transportation, more stores, museums, etc.	getting close to nature and fresh air
feature 2: environment	more pollution	clean and quiet
feature 3: job opportunities	more companies and factories	farming, fishing, and lumbering (伐木)

Exercise B

2. Also/Similarly/Likewise   3. Although   4. while
5. the same as   6. different from

Exercise C

I.

The topic sentence:

Living in a city and living in the country differ in the following three ways.

The supporting ideas:

feature 1: conveniences

Living in a city, one can enjoy all the conveniences, such as mass transportation and shopping malls, while traveling around or doing the shopping is relatively difficult for those who live in the country.

feature 2: environment

Unlike the quiet and peaceful countryside, the hustle and bustle of a city often makes its residents feel stressed, which can affect their health.

feature 3: pace of life

The pace of life in a city is much faster than that in the country.

feature 4: job opportunities

When it comes to job opportunities, the country can't compare with a city because there are many stores, companies, and government institutions in a city where jobs can be found more easily.

The concluding sentence:

All in all, there are advantages and disadvantages of living in a city or in the country, and the choice of where to live depends on one's personal needs.

Transitional words or phrases:

first, while, unlike, in addition, however, all in all

II.

The point-by-point method.

Exercise D

First, their ages are not the same. Generally speaking, college graduates are four to seven years older than high school graduates. The former are about 22, while the latter are around 18. In addition, compared to college graduates, high school graduates tend to be more enthusiastic about graduation because it symbolizes their growing independence. Most parents allow high school graduates to study in other towns or even in other countries because they are no longer considered children. However, unlike high school graduates, college graduates are under greater pressure because they need to decide whether to find a job or pursue further study. Now, there are much fewer job opportunities than before, which adds to the burdens college graduates face. So, it seems, based on these considerations, that, college graduates and high school graduates have little in common.

Unit 20

Exercise A

Effect 1: health problems
Effect 2: psychological problems
Effect 3: social problems
Cause 1: lack of sleep
Cause 2: lack of exercise
Cause 3: eating disorder

Exercise B

2. because of   3. therefore   4. so   5. As a result

Exercise C

Effect 1: major wildfires
Effect 2: severe changes to the earth's climate
Effect 3: the ice surrounding the North Pole and the South Pole has begun to melt

Global warming has already affected our planet in many serious ways. It is actually making the world's weather conditions much worse. For one thing, unusually hot weather has caused major wildfires in the United States, Indonesia, and Australia. For another, as the planet warms up, the ice surrounding the North Pole and the South Pole has begun to melt, causing the planet's sea level to rise. If this continues, some big cities like London, New York, and Taipei might be underwater by the end of this century. In addition, global warming may also be responsible for causing many severe changes to the planet's climate. Scientists think of all the recent huge floods and droughts as evidence of this severe climate change. Thus, it is essential that we take immediate action to deal with global warming before it is too late to save the earth.

Unit 21

Exercise A

O	I agree that students should wear school uniforms.
R	If all the students wear the same uniforms, it will help develop a stronger group spirit.
E	Take myself, for example. Whenever I put on my school uniform, I automatically start to act better in public when I go out because I don't want to disgrace my school.
O	Wearing uniforms lets students identify with their school, so the policy of mandatory uniforms should not be abandoned.

Exercise B

2. what's more   3. Another reason
4. it was my belief that   5. As for me

Exercise C

1.

O	Facebook actually makes more distance between people because it doesn't help them strengthen relationships with their friends.
R	Facebook often leads to the end of a friendship because many people use it as a tool to vent (發洩) their bad emotions.
E	Some people impulsively post rude or even hateful messages on Facebook when they are arguing with their friends.

O	Facebook makes people grow further apart instead of bringing them together.

2.

Though the social networking service, Facebook, enables millions of people set up connections with their friends, I don't think it actually helps build up relationships among friends. As a matter of fact, Facebook often leads to the end of a friendship because many people use it as a tool to vent their bad emotions. People sometimes post hateful messages on Facebook in the heat of anger when they are having problems with their friends. Even if they regret their words at once, it is too late because the update will have already been viewed and possibly shared by a number of mutual friends. As a result, their relationship might never be the same as it used to be. In short, Facebook creates more distance between people instead of bringing them together.

Unit 22

Exercise

The pie chart above shows how an average house uses electricity in the U.K. More than half of the electricity is used for heating rooms and water. About eighteen percent of the electricity is consumed by ovens, kettles, and washing machines. The rest is equally divided into two parts. One is used in lighting, TV and radio, and the other is in the use of vacuum cleaners, food mixer, and electric tools.

Unlike the U.K., Taiwan is very hot and humid. Since the climates in these two areas are drastically different, how electricity is used differs as well. In Taiwan, air-conditioners and dehumidifiers consume a large proportion of electricity. Thirty percent is consumed for other electric appliances such as TVs, refrigerators, and washing machines. Ten percent is used for lighting. Last but not least, since computers are used a lot in Taiwan, many families have several computers. Thus, the electricity consumption by computers also plays a part.

Unit 23

Exercise A

1.
(A) Growing up means becoming mature and responsible.
(B) Growing up means not making complaints without any reason.
(C) Growing up means showing concern for others.

2.
(A) A true friend is one who offers help without asking anything in return.
(B) A true friend shares both joy and sorrow.
(C) A true friend will not betray you no matter what happens.

Exercise B

1. In other words
2. For instance/For example; In addition/Besides
3. That is to say; However/Nevertheless; For instance/For example

Exercise C

Happiness

Happiness is a feeling of being pleased and satisfied. With such a feeling, our mind is filled with comfort, peace and love. This feeling has nothing to do with fame, power, wealth or status.

Happiness is a feeling everyone can find. It's a state of mind. People with fame or power may be afraid of losing it. Rich business people are busy promoting their businesses and worrying about their businesses going down. They can't enjoy the real feeling of happiness. However, a child goes into ecstasies when given a toy. A person has the sense of happiness when having a dinner with the family members. We enjoy the feeling of happiness when we see the beautiful scenery, listen to music, or receive a call from our friends. Something simple and ordinary may be the source of real happiness.

Happiness lies not in what we have but how we think. For example, when we are in trouble, we may choose to feel sad and live in misery, or to be optimistic and face it. In a state of happiness, we tend to look on the bright side, which will make our life even happier. Happiness is also contagious. Our happiness may pass on to others easily and rapidly. Happiness is what makes our life worth living.

Unit 24

Exercise A

2.

(A) As the saying goes, "Procrastination is the thief of time." Putting off things that we should do is just a way to waste more time.

(B) If we are in the habit of putting things off, we will be less likely to get things done on time, which may give others a very bad impression.

(C) Habit is second nature. Therefore, we should break the bad habit, and the sooner the better.

3.

(A) If we face failure bravely, we will try again and again. Thus, we learn more lessons, which become our knowledge and form the foundation of our success. Success belongs to those who are not afraid of failure.

(B) We gain lessons and experience from failure as well as from success. We learn what will work and what won't work.

(C) No pains, no gains. It is also true that there is no success without experiencing failure. How Edison invented the electric lamp serves a good example.

Exercise B

1. Also/What's worse; Worst of all

2. First; Besides; Therefore

3. because of; In addition to; What's more; In addition; Best of all; because

Exercise C

1.

We must all say "No" to drugs for a number of reasons. First, taking drugs is against the law. Those who break the law will never escape punishment. So, they may end up in prison or rehab (勒戒所). Second, taking drugs not only undermines one's health but ruins one's life. Once a person is addicted to drugs, his

or her physical and mental health begins to deteriorate. What's worse, since this person needs a lot of money for the drugs, he or she is likely to steal, rob, or even commit murder to get enough money.

In fact, the rates of criminal behavior, violence, and fatal accidents among drug users are much higher than those in the general population. This in turn costs the country a large amount of money every year. This is the money that could be used to benefit the public.

In a word, taking drugs is a stupid thing to do. If we don't say "No" to drugs now, there will be no future for us to say "Yes."

2.

There are many people that have had an influence on me, but the one who has influenced me the most is my friend Jack.

Jack is my neighbor and he is now a college student. There are a number of reasons that I admire him. First, he is very talented. He can play several musical instruments, including the guitar, the piano, and the drums. He likes to compose music and write songs, and he has written more than thirty songs already! The songs he wrote are fun to listen to, and they have some deep meanings, too. Second, Jack is always willing to help people. He spends most of his free time volunteering in the community. He helps children to develop an interest in music and teaches them how to play the guitar for free. Even though he spends so much time volunteering, he is still able to do well academically. It is hard to believe that such a young man has achieved so much already.

Because of Jack, I have started learning how to play the guitar. I've been even trying to compose music like he does. Also, inspired by him, I have decided to join a volunteer group. I want to help other people, too. Jack is just the kind of person that I want to be. I hope that someday I will be like him and have a positive influence on other people.

Unit 25

Exercise A

2.
(A) Overweight people are more likely to suffer from diabetes and heart disease.
(B) Obese people have more bad habits that make them less healthy. For example, they eat a lot of snacks.
(C) Obese people tend to be clumsy so they are more likely to have accidents.

3.
(A) She always wears a smile and seldom loses her temper.
(B) She often spends her free time working as a volunteer in hospital.
(C) She volunteers to clean up the beach.

4.
(A) He has no sympathy with other people.
(B) He always puts himself in the first place.
(C) He cares nothing but what benefits him.

Exercise B

1. For instance/For example; while
2. For one thing; Therefore; Besides/In addition; Best of all
3. For one thing; For another; Furthermore

Exercise C

1.
The Topic Sentence:
Life isn't always about saying "Yes" to everything.
The Supporting Ideas:
① I had to practice for the volleyball game.
② My friends asked me to go to a party with them.
③ I refused to go to the party, but they understood why I made this choice.
The Conclusion:
Sometimes, saying no is the right thing to do.

2.

Life isn't always about saying "Yes" to everything. We have to think seriously about the consequences. If we promise someone to do something, we should keep the promise; otherwise, we will lose credibility. In reality, sometimes saying "No" is a wise decision.

I can remember one time that I said "no" to my friends. A school volleyball game was approaching, and we had to practice every weekend. But one weekend, my friends asked me to go to a party with them. It was an afternoon party, and going to it would mean missing volleyball practice. It was a hard decision to make, but in the end, I said "no" to my friends, and told them I had to practice volleyball that day. I was surprised that they didn't get angry. Instead, they completely supported my choice.

Through this experience, I learn it is not rude to say "no" to others when it is necessary. Sometimes, it is the right thing to do.

Unit 26

Exercise A

How to Prepare for an Interview

Being interviewed is an event everyone will face at some time in life. It may be an interview for a college or a job. Being well-prepared is sure to increase your chances of having a successful outcome of the interview.

The first step is to do the research and make sure you understand what the interview is all about. Collect as much information as possible so that you will get an idea about the questions that may be asked. Remember that a boss is unlikely to hire a person who knows nothing about the company. Besides, what you wear and how you look are important. Be sure to dress properly for the interview. It would be better to dress a little more formally than not. After all, an interview is an important occasion. If you dress too casually, it may suggest that you don't care enough about the interview. During the interview, you should be confident, sincere and honest. Don't talk too much or too little. If you don't know the answer, be honest about it. Just make a brief apology and promise to the interviewers that you will try to find the answer.

To sum up, making a good impression is important. Being well-prepared will increase your chances of success. Even if you do not succeed at the first time, the experience itself is a valuable lesson.

Exercise B

How to Plan a Party

There are times we have to hold a party such as birthdays, reunions and other occasions for celebration. As a result, knowing how to plan a party is necessary.

There are some steps to follow. First of all, you need to decide on who or how many you want to invite. Depending on the reason why the party is held, you may invite your family members, relatives, friends, or classmates. Next, you need to decide when to hold the party. Generally speaking, weekends are better choices, since most people don't have to go to work or school. Next, you have to decide where to hold the party. If you decide to hold the party at a restaurant, you must be sure of the number of the attendants and make a reservation. To be efficient, you can first ask by telephone to get a rough idea. After these are settled down, you can start to send out the invitations. Some restaurants offer a free party-invitation system on their websites. In that case, you only need to type in the e-mail addresses of your guests, and the system will send out the invitations to them automatically. Later, it will inform you about who has accepted your invitation and who hasn't.

In fact, planning a party is not as difficult as we think it is. It only takes some time and effort to organize it.

Unit 27

Exercise A

2.

(1) Stop eating junk food.

(2) Change the diet and take regular exercise.

(3) Consult a doctor, if necessary.

3.

(1) Find out the reason for feeling frustrated.

(2) Talk to teachers, friends and parents about your problem(s).

(3) Ask counseling experts for help, if necessary.

4.

(1) The government should set up reservations for rare species.

(2) Make laws to punish those who kill or hurt rare animals and plants.

(3) Forbid or limit the number of the people who visit the habitats of endangered species.

Exercise B

I.

1. According to   2. In general   3. For example

4. Most importantly

II.

1. The toothbrush can harbor bacteria. These germs come from the mouth and can accumulate in toothbrushes over time.

2. We can rinse the toothbrush thoroughly with tap water after use, making sure to remove any toothpaste and debris. We should store our toothbrush in an upright position, and let it air dry. Most importantly, we should not share toothbrushes.

Exercise C

I used to be shy, not talking much with my classmates. Therefore, I was categorized as an arrogant and self-centered student. Little by little, I was isolated from my classmates. Most of the time, I was alone and lonely in class. How I wished to laugh with my classmates and make fun of each other.

I decided to make a change. The first thing I learned was the importance of wearing a smile. I found that a smile indeed worked like magic. My classmates also showed friendliness by greeting me with smiles. Some of them even began to talk to me. Besides, I tried to show concern for my classmates. Whenever I found someone in trouble or having difficulty with school work, I always offered my help and received thanks and won friendship in return.

Now, I spend a lot of time with my friends. We

talk about our secrets, sharing joy and sorrow with each other. I am considered wonderful and thoughtful. I feel pleased and blessed to have so many good friends around.

Unit 28

Exercise

Topic: My Thoughts on *Anne Frank's Diary*

1.

The Topic Sentence:

Anne Frank's Diary, written by a girl younger than me, has touched my heart.

The Supporting Ideas:

① a brief summary of the story

② the part that impresses me the most

③ what I have learned from the story

2.

　　Anne Frank's Diary, written by a girl younger than me, has deeply touched my heart. Anne Frank got the diary as a birthday present at 13 when she was still leading a normal life. However, things changed completely after the Nazis took over and Hitler made strict laws against the Jews. The Frank family had no choice but to hide in the Secret Annex. Anne started writing her diary as a young teenager, and she matured physically and emotionally through the two years of hiding. What impressed me most was that even though she was confined to a small place, she still showed appreciation for being able to stay with her family and could also express concern for those who suffered outside. Anne was compassionate about human suffering, and to her last breath she never gave up hope. How many of us who are more fortunate are as grateful and compassionate as Anne was?

Unit 29

Exercise A

1.

For →

Written reports might require students to think more deeply and consider issues from more than one side, instead of just memorizing a correct answer.

Against →

They may simply copy material directly from the Internet to complete the report. It would be difficult to be sure if the ideas are their own.

2.

For →

There is no denying that the smartphone helps us a lot. It can provide a lot of information about every aspect of life. What's better, it is available at any time.

Against →

Teenagers often spend much more time on smartphones than on the relationship with their family and their schoolwork. This results in the gap in communication and in the negligence in their studies. What's worse, staring at the screens for a long time hurts the eyes.

3.

For →

Uniforms represent group identity. Besides, it is not necessary for the students to spend time considering what to wear.

Against →

Wearing uniforms can't meet the expectation of girls and boys of the golden age. They think wearing casual clothes makes their life more colorful. Most importantly, they will learn how to dress themselves properly.

Exercise B

1. Besides　2. For example　3. More importantly

4. On the other hand

Exercise C

　　Joining a school club is a good idea for senior high school students because they have reached a stage in their lives where their own interests begin to develop.

　　There are many advantages of belonging to a school club. For one thing, students may discover something they are really interested in outside the regular curriculum. There are clubs for almost every kind of activity, such as photography clubs, bands, choirs, and street dance groups. There are clubs devoted to drama, broadcasting, skating, swimming, and movie studies; of course there are clubs for every kind of ball games. A club is also a place where students can develop their abilities in the specific area. Take the guitar club which my brother joined, for example. He not only learned the basics, but also gained a better appreciation for playing and listening to music. Last but not least, a club is a place to make new friends. Clubs and activities give students from different classes a chance to meet and to talk about their common interests.

Joining school clubs provides students with an escape from the pressure of courses and tests. It also offers them a way to develop more of their potential and open up a new world for them.

Unit 30

Exercise A

category 1: narrative
category 2: descriptive
category 3: persuasive
category 4: expository

Exercise B

2. Second   3. For example   4. Lastly

Exercise C

1. There are three types of shoppers, price shoppers, value shoppers, and luxury shoppers.
2. Regular exercise, calorie control, and surgery are three most effective ways to lose weight.

Exercise D

Scientists have categorized volcanoes into three main categories: active, dormant, and extinct. An active volcano is one that is erupting now, has erupted in the last 10,000 years or may erupt again in the near future. A dormant volcano is a volcano that has not erupted in historical times, but for which there is still the possibility of future eruption. An extinct volcano is one that hasn't erupted for thousands of years and has almost no likelihood of another eruption. The above classification is mainly based on a volcano's eruptive pattern.

Unit 31

Exercise A

Once Upon a time, there was a shepherd boy. Bored by his monotonous job, he often played tricks to liven himself up. One day, for example, he ran around shouting, "Wolf! Wolf! A wolf is eating the lambs!" even though there was no wolf to be found.

Hearing the boy's shouts, the villagers stopped what they were doing and ran to save the boy and the sheep. When the boy saw how easy it was to fool them, he was very pleased with himself. He played this trick over and over until the villagers no longer believed him.

One day, though, a wolf did appear. The boy cried, "Wolf! Wolf!" again and again. No one came for help. The wolf had a feast of sheep that day, and the boy narrowly escaped being devoured.

Exercise B

The Dragon Boat Festival falls on the fifth day of the fifth month of the lunar calendar. It is one of the most important Chinese festivals. The festival originated from a patriotic poet named Chu Yuan. Out of jealousy, his rivals spoke ill of him and caused him to lose the respect of the emperor. In his sorrow, Chu Yuan threw himself into the Mi Lo River. On hearing this, the local people rushed into their boats to search for him while throwing rice into the waters to keep the fish from devouring his body. Now, it has become a traditional custom for people to eat rice dumplings and hold boat races on this day. Besides, it is also considered a day for protection against evil. By doing some traditional customs, people hope that it can make everything go well in the year.

Unit 32

Exercise A

I was born in 1835 to a weaver's family in Scotland and expected to follow my father's profession. However, Industrial Revolution destroyed my father's business and we had to leave for America for new possibilities.

In 1848, we arrived in Pittsburgh, the iron-manufacturing center of the country. Life was hard. I took odd jobs at a cotton factory and worked as a messenger boy in the telegraph office. I was often asked to deliver messages to the city theater, where I would stay to watch plays and spent most of my leisure hours in a small library.

After the civil war, I saw great potential in the iron industry and devoted myself to the replacement of wooden bridges with iron ones. I earned a fortune. Furthermore, I introduced a new steel refining process to convert iron into steel. By 1900, my steel company produced more of the metal than all of Great Britain.

However, I often felt uneasy about my business life. I didn't like to put my thought to making more money. Sometimes I even felt ashamed of myself. The strong desire for spiritual pursuit led me to sell my company and retire at the age of 64.

After retirement, I turned my attention to giving away my fortune. Instead of donating money to individuals, I began to establish public libraries, sponsor cultural, educational and scientific institutions. I think in this way, I can help people help themselves and the benefit would go on and on.

Exercise B

My name is Jia-Ling Yang. I was born and raised in Taiwan. I am currently a student at Xin-Yi Senior High School. Being the only child in my family, I have been raised as the focus of my parents' love and attention. However, this does not mean that they spoiled me. Instead, they have taught me how to behave and fostered warmth and enthusiasm in me. I am lucky to have many friends, and I have to thank my parents for that.

My interests range from music and sports to reading and writing. Among these interests, I am especially interested in the wonders of nature. When I was a child, I used to ask questions about natural phenomena, such as the sun, the moon, rainbow and the dew. My father, who was a physics teacher, would explain to me with patience. I was always listening

attentively. My father also told me that a lot of phenomena in nature had something to do with physics. Since I went to senior high school, I have been even more fascinated with physics, hoping to explore more of nature. I joined many activities concerning observing and studying the nature. I also took part in scientific competitions and won several prizes. I was determined to major in physics in college.

By putting my heart into this field, I will be able to make a concrete contribution to society while pursuing a topic that interests me greatly. After graduation from college, I will continue with my studies. I believe that my background, experience, determination, and effort will make me a good candidate for NCTU. I do hope that I have the opportunity to be granted admission.

Unit 33

Exercise

I.

Introduction	reasons for applying to the Japanese Department	
Body: Study Plan	Short-term Goal	improve my Japanese, get a part-time job
	Mid-term Goal	take required and elective courses, join clubs
	Long-term Goal	work as an interpreter and translator, work in a trading company
Conclusion	emphasize intelligence, motivation, and appreciation for the opportunity	

II.

In the global village, being able to speak different languages is the best way to help spread culture around the world. Among all the languages of the world, Japanese is the one that I am most interested in.

It is not only because Japan is a highly developed country but because Japan has a great influence on Taiwan. In addition, your department offers in-depth courses in modern and classical Japanese literature and also allows students to take courses offered by other departments. A good foundation like this will offer me a big step on the road to becoming an interpreter and translator and working in a trading company. My goals are as follows:

Short-term Goal (from now to the beginning of school)

During these five months before school starts, I will work on my Japanese proficiency by learning more vocabulary, reading Japanese novels, and watching Japanese TV programs. I also plan to go on a working holiday in Japan during the coming summer vacation. Whatever job I find, I will have the opportunity to sharpen my Japanese and learn more about Japanese culture.

Mid-term Goal (four years in college)

After fulfilling the general education requirements, I plan to put more effort into refining my skills in oral interpretation and translation. Apart from the courses in the Japanese Department, I am going to take commerce and business courses to improve my job prospects. As for extracurricular activities, I am certainly going to join the Japanese Club to immerse myself as deeply as I can in the living cultures of Japan.

Long-term Goals (after graduation)

After graduation, I don't plan to go directly into graduate school. I plan to find a job in a Japanese company first. Hopefully, by the time my spoken Japanese and commercial skills will be attractive to employers and can afford me some chances for advancement in the job. In my free time, I will continue to translate Japanese novels or TV programs on a part-time basis. I will also like to try oral interpretation if I get the opportunity.

Write Right 讓所有文章都 不NG！

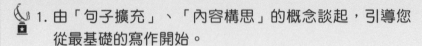

本書特色：

1. 由「句子擴充」、「內容構思」的概念談起，引導您從最基礎的寫作開始。

2. 提點常見的寫作錯誤，如標點符號、時態等，替您打下紮實的基本功。

3. 介紹常見文體，包括記敘文、描寫文、論說文、應用文等，讓您充分學習。

4. 補充自傳、讀書計畫等寫作技巧，幫助您為生涯規劃加分。

5. 循序漸進引導，按部就班練習，自學、教學都不NG！

題本與解答本不分售

80109G

三民網路書店
www.sanmin.com.tw